Tammy

S0-AAM-518

Lostman's
River

Gulf

of

Mexico

Whitewater
Bay

Cape Sable

campsite

mangrove swamp

sawgrass marsh

Florida Bay

A NOVEL BY
R.R. Knudson

YOU
ARE
THE
RAIN

Published by
Dell Publishing Co., Inc.
1 Dag Hammarskjold Plaza
New York, New York 10017

YOU
ARE
THE
RAIN

JUNE 1st

"Rain!"

"Ugh!"

"That's rain on the windshield!"

"Swell. What'll we do now?"

I felt the car sideslip a little as Mrs. Regan
reached to turn on the wipers. They left a blotchy
trail through which she peered nearsightedly at the
sky. "Rain. Oh my. We'd better go back, girls,"
she said, coasting us to a stop.

Chicken lady. Like daughter, like mother, I
thought, hauling myself up from a backseat slouch
for a view of this big thunderhead. "June, drop
your dumb book so I can see the . . ." Oh brother!
Across the field a giant sprinkler moved slowly on
its rollers, watering beans and tomatoes. I pointed
at the machine. "Some rain! It's called 'irrigation'
by the farmers around here. Catchy word." I let
out a disgusted bunch of breath and reslouched.
Some rain!

"From the same root as 'rain.' 'Rigāre, irrigāre,
irrigation . . .'"

June's mouse voice was drowned by engine noise

as our crowded station wagon lurched over gravel
shoulders. Along in here we should turn southwest
again, I thought, feeling the tires hug hot tar. Let's
get there. Let's do it.

"June, dear. What were you saying? About the
rain?" Mrs. Regan absent-mindedly turned her
head to look at her precious poet.

"Nothing, Mother." Whispered.

I caught Rollie's "ugh" glance in the rear-view
mirror just as the tires thumped once, twice, and
the car veered into the left lane. Mrs. Regan hit
the brakes, wobbled us back across the double line,
and stopped again.

"Oh, dear, I did strike that poor snake. I didn't
see. I swerved. Really. I tried to miss it."

"Way to go. Great shot there, Mrs. R." Rollie
shook her red ponytail and held a thumb up.
"Bravo." We all turned to watch the death wiggle.
A dark wavy line played across the rear window.
"Squish city, fang baby," hollered Rollie.

"How terribly messy," groaned Lalla.

"Hope she was pregnant. Wipe 'em all out in
one fell whamp." Rollie laughed. "A hundred po-
tential killers—bam."

"How ghastly," moaned Lalla.

"Writhe, fangy, writhe!" Rollie writhed some
too. She looped her long arms around her neck
and coughed. She rolled her eyes back.

The dark line straightened and lay still. I called
out, "Another water moccasin bites the macadam.
Pity him. Or her." I put my hand over my heart
and faked a sniffle. "Honk the horn. Summon the

buzzards." I craned my neck for a final tail jerk. "June, quick, write a death poem."

"Yeah, Junie, a poem of mourning: 'Hiss no longer, o ye gentle biter, riddled with tire tracks . . .'" Rollie laughed some more.

June closed her book. "How might you feel back there in his place?" she asked quietly. "Deathdancing on a public road in front of a bunch of . . . of . . .'" I left off my snake vigil and looked at her. Skin like a red-spotted newt now. Gritted teeth. Eyes sad gray. A kill-joy. But no one paid any attention, not even her mother, who stared over the field.

Rollie said, "That can't be a moccasin, Crash. We're too far from water. The first sloughs aren't until just before we enter the park. I've never seen a cottonmouth road-kill at this end of Route 27." She held her hands apart a foot. "Besides, he's too short."

Rollie should know, so I said, "Back up, Mrs. Regan. Let's have a look at your victim. He must be dead. We're safe." June shuddered next to me as the car rolled backward and—of course—over the snake again.

"Gotcha twice, vicious viper. To make sure." Rollie hopped out of the front seat.

"Oh dear, did I hit him again?" Mrs. Regan asked an almost empty car, for by now we stood around the body exclaiming, examining.

"Quite a complex skin pattern on the corpse, wouldn't you say?"

"Ick. He's gooey."

"Check those beady eyes. Cruel."

"Never mind the eyes. Check those fangs. He could munch you good."

"*If* he were alive." I bent down to touch the rattles. "Worse than anything, he's cold. So cold." I shook the tail. Not a sound. "Rollie, do you collect these? Want to cut them off?"

"Too small. I'm into diamondbacks—the giant stuff. This fellow's rattles aren't worth the trouble. He's only a nothing pygmy rattlesnake."

I flipped about half of him over. Twisted belly up, he seemed a harmless reptile. I examined the cream-colored stomach skin. Black spots mingled with faint traces of red. "Not much blood in a snake, I guess. I told you he's cold." I kicked the body into some weeds and wiped my hands on my shorts. "It will take more than a pygmy's poison to finish off Crash Adams," I announced to anyone listening.

A soft gasp—or snort—came from the car. June? Her mother? Who cared! Rollie climbed onto the tailgate and organized a nest for herself among the tent bags. "Crash could bite anything back with those big teeth of hers," she said, then, "Sit with me, pal. We'll lay our plans." She shoved over some canoe paddles, our grub box, several army blankets. "Here's room for the three of us, Lalla. Let the boob ride in front."

"Don't fall off, girls," warned Mrs. Regan as we bumped away from the murder scene.

Clumps of palm trees jiggled by, then some pines and a fruit stand advertising avocados and tropical

wonder-juices: mangoes, guavas, passion fruit. I slid
farther into the car and looked for the poet. She
must be lying on the back seat. I nudged Rollie.
"Baby June seems to have disappeared. We won't
have to push her buggy this week after all." In the
window I could see reflected pale hands holding a
book up high: ꙅməoꟼ bnɒ ꙅɟəoꟼ

Rollie saw, too. "Attagirl, Junie. You can really
pick 'em. The very book we'll need in the darkest
Everglades."

"Sure, in case we get lost. Just open up to any
page and presto, we're home free." I snorted back
at the Regans.

"June baby, read us a sample. Something nice in
'Trees' or 'Oh Captain, My Captain.' Maybe 'Little
Boy Blue.' We're waiting excitedly." Under her
breath Rollie added, "After that you better chuck
the whole bunch of them in a canal." She nodded
at the ditch we'd just crossed. "You might find
cottonmouths there, Crash. And rattlers over in
that canebreak—gangs of them. Coral snakes, too,
under those logs by the fence." She pointed.
"They're related to the cobra."

"Never heard of . . . Reef coral? None in that
field over there. Not this far inland."

"Coral color. Bands of red, black, and pinkish
yellow—coral. Small snake. Two-footer. Skinny."
Rollie made a Life Saver O with her thumb and
index finger. "But deadly, deadlier than . . . Fatal
a lot. One drop of poison . . ."

Lalla shivered and said, "Just keep it up, you
two, and I won't set foot out of this car. Camping

in the 'Glades will be brutal enough without snakes to fear."

" 'Sweet is the swamp with its secrets' " came a mouse voice over the back seat.

"Everglades aren't entirely swamps . . ." started Rollie.

"You asked for a poem. Won't you please listen." June sat up and looked at us.

"So we're listening," I said, cupping hands around my ears. "Read up."

" 'Sweet is the swamp with its secrets / Until we meet a snake / 'Tis then we sigh for houses / And our departure take.' "

Rollie's face got as red as her hair. She pretended to throw up. "Poetry gets me sick, with words like *'tis* and *sweet*. No one really talks that way. Ech."

"Poetry isn't talk," June said quietly, her face splotchy, her eyes narrowed. "It's better. Magic, really. Besides, Emily Dickinson wrote those words almost a hundred years ago, when people said *'tis.*"

"Emily! Dickinson! She's my very worst poet of them all. Prissy old maid with her starchy petticoats and tacky cameo." I banged open the campstove and turned both knobs to "on." A hiss of gas filled our nest. "Lean back here, June. Take a deep sniff. Might clear your head."

She ignored me and read to the poem's end. I turned off the butane. I caught the last lines as we entered the park: "A snake is summer's treason / And guile is where it goes."

A mustached ranger collected the entrance fee

from Mrs. Regan. "Welcome to Everglades National Park, ladies." He handed a green pamphlet through the window. "Any questions?"

"We're part of the wilderness waterway group," began Mrs. Regan.

"Trying to connect with the rest of our crew at noon," Rollie butted in.

The ranger stooped and ran his eyes around the inside of our station wagon. "I see you're well equipped." He straightened up. "That pale kid going along?" he asked. "Better cover her with suntan lotion." He walked back to the tailgate. "You three appear hearty enough."

"We're hearty all right," said Rollie in her tough voice. "We'll storm up that waterway like Olympic canoers." She moved her hands in rapid paddle motions.

The ranger took off his hat, fanned himself, looked up at the sky, then down at us. "Might get a tad of rain later on."

"We won't melt. We'll keep on stroking," I said.

"A lot can happen in a week to take the wind out of your sails, young lady. Or put it in!" He seemed amused. I wasn't.

Quick as a bunny Rollie said, "We aren't sailing. We're paddling."

He smiled crookedly. He tipped his hat till it strained against its chin strap. He returned to the driver's window. "If they're all as fierce as that big redhead you've got there—well, gangway wilderness!" He pointed straight ahead. "Follow this main park road right down to Flamingo. Thirty-eight miles. The rest of your, uh, paddle-girls will be gathering at the marina."

The car jerked out from under the sheltered entrance-station and along Route 27 again. West, then southwest. Past park headquarters. Past the Anhinga Trail. Past Lone Pine Key. Past Pa-hay-okee Overlook. By now the sun, almost directly overhead, glared hard at us. Some rain! I thought. Rollie said, "We're in for a sweaty time, looks like." She had read my mind, as usual.

"Let's be sure we're assigned to the same canoe, Rollie. We'll make a race of it."

"Include me too," said Lalla. "I'll lie in the bottom and dangle my toes overboard while you two muscles fan me."

Past Mahogany Hummock while we planned our camp dinners: Big. Past Nine Mile Pond while Rollie lectured on the proper size to build fires: Big, to keep insects at bay. Past West Lake Trail while we discussed our tent: Too small for more than the three of us. Past Snake Bight Canal, where we each whipped out our first-aid boxes and named off the goodies. Only Lalla's contained a snake-bite kit. "Who needs it," I said at Rowdy Bend Road. In a minute I heard flopping boards as we crossed a low bridge. Right now, Flamingo. Ahead nothing but blue water.

We rolled up to a line of royal palms that arched the boat slips. We stopped between two other station wagons and waved to our fellow trippers, who lolled among duffles and sleeping bags. No canoes in sight. They must be in the water already, under the dock. Another furnace-faced ranger began barking instructions, so we joined the semi-circle forming around him.

"And girls, keep a sharp eye for deadheads."

I looked over the nine of us, hoping to single out loafers before we stroked off. A stout bunch here. Members of Nature, Inc. Only the poet seemed to qualify as deadbeat. I pinched Rollie and pointed to June. "Not that sort of deadhead, pal," whispered Rollie. *"Deadheads.* Logs so water-soaked that they float just under the surface, out of sight. Ram one once and you'll find out. Bust a hole through the hull."

"And keep well sprayed with repellent. Mosquitoes are in season hereabouts."

"When aren't they swarming in Florida?" I asked Rollie, hoping I'd remembered my Off. She made some slapping motions, winked at me, and said, "I'll use mud and pine tar. Better than that canned stuff."

"Okay, each of you hold up your compass. No one gets into a folboat without a compass and life vest." Hands shot high, even a pale one. The ranger walked around tapping crystals, shaking needles. Rollie draped her new black-rimmed compass over her forehead like a jewel on a rajah. Its luminous points glowed milky emerald. "Hope you can read it" is all he said to her.

"If not, she'll navigate by the stars," I bragged as

he fumbled around with my old-fashioned compass in its cracked case. "She'll sight along landmarks by day. She knows these 'Glades better than . . ."

"You'd never find your way back to camp with this old thing, Blondie. It's maybe a hundred degrees off. Kaput." He shook water drops from my compass. He squinted at the yellow dial and grouched, "You haven't complied with regulations, my girl. You must stay here—go home, I mean."

Rollie kicked a fallen palm frond at the guy. "Like heck she will, Mr. Rulebook. Crash paddles with me. We're together all the way." I slung an arm around her neck.

"She can't go without a compass," he said again, quite simply.

"Crash can use my compass," said June. I felt a cold round object slip into my hand. A small cold hand folded my fingers over the lanyard. "I never cared to go anyway," she whispered.

And we don't want you either, I thought. We only asked you because we needed your mother's station wagon for all this stuff. But I pressed the compass back into her hand.

Rollie didn't give up on that guy. She argued. She pleaded. She threatened. She got pushier and pushier. Her freckles puffed out, and not from the sun, which had disappeared behind a small cloud. Finally she tried logic, shouting, "Lookit! Me and Crash will be in the same boat, understand? Won't this waterproof beauty guide us both home, if worst comes to worst?" She whirled her compass on its chain. It grazed his nose.

The ranger wiped his crimson brow on a shirt cuff. His lips started to form "N—O" just as June leveled her eyes on him and said, " 'Adrift! A little boat adrift! / And night is coming down! / Will no one guide a little boat / Unto the nearest town?' "

"Whatever are you mumbling about?" he asked, staring down at our reject.

"A poem. I'm saying a poem. By Emily Dickinson. Two more verses to come: 'Our little boat gave up its strife / And gurgled down and down . . .' "

The ranger reddened up even more. "Okay, okay, *you* win. Two on a compass. Four on a life jacket. Six in a folboat. Anything but poetry. Kicks. Scratches. Slaps. Bites . . ."

"Verse is worse," agreed Rollie, joining sides with the ranger now he'd given in.

"That's a fact, Red." He smiled at her. "Now listen to today's weather report. Expected high, ninety degrees. About the same for expected low. Humidity, sixty percent. Virtually no wind. Maybe a little breeze tomorrow. Maybe some showers tonight or tomorrow. Is anyone taking a radio?"

Lalla held hers up by its fat antenna. "I couldn't miss Elton John for a solid week. I'd go swamp crazy." Cheers broke out for our swinger.

"Okay, girls. Tune into WINK every morning at eight-twenty for the marine weather forecast. Dial twelve forty." He smiled again, this time at Lalla. "Not your kind of music, but listen anyway." Suddenly he grew serious. "A possible storm may be forming near the Dominican Republic. Nothing to fret about way down in the Caribbean. No danger to us this far northwest, at least for days—a week." Then he smiled broadly at the group. "If the Park Service thought there'd be the slightest likelihood of a hurricane—well, we'd turn you all home. I don't mean to frighten you."

"You haven't," I said, squinting at the blue sky, then down at Buttonwood Canal, smooth as bathwater. "Don't you know what we Miamians say about hurricanes?

> June
> Too soon
> July
> Stand by
> August
> Look out you must
> September
> Remember
> October
> All over

We're safe. June's too soon."

Rollie whooped, "Especially poet June, the goon," and we laughed.

Our ranger said, "More rhymes yet! So you're poets, too," looking at Rollie and me, then around. "A group of poets? The Wilderness Poetry Society? Rhymettes?" He didn't wait for an answer. "In any case, this is only the second all-girl tour we've allowed from Flamingo. We need to be certain you're prepared."

With that he took our group leader, Miss Konecky, to the far end of a pier. We couldn't hear his private instructions. Instead we noticed his gestures —at mangrove trees along Florida Bay, at pelicans atop a houseboat, at her wristwatch and whistle, and finally at a pile of canvas bags near the snack bar. "He's telling her he'll buy us a parting creamsicle, one for the road," said Rollie expectantly. But nothing doing. As they walked toward us again he unrolled a large paper from a tube.

"Okay, you girls, assemble the folboats while I outline your coarse for Miss Konecky," he called, bending to spread a map on the ground. They put their heads together over the yellow, green, and blue shapes on the Bermuda grass.

"Folboats? What? Where?" Rollie broke for the dock.

"Over there. Okay, I'd better show you." The ranger hustled us all to pavement beside the snack bar and began quickly unzipping bags, dumping their contents at our feet. "Red, I thought you knew about these boats. Aren't you the local hotshot?" He sorted through some short aluminum poles. One at a time, he fit these into notched pieces of plywood. Within seconds this framework became a hull, every part locked in place by metal hasps. Astonished, we watched as he shoved the frame into a long vinyl case shaped like a canoe. He secured the bottom on its aluminum hooks, inserted two seats in their grooves, and said, "Unfolded boat. From bag to water in ten minutes."

Rollie pranced delightedly around this craft. "Whoopie, a kayak. Safer than a canoe any day.

Rides lower in the water. Can't turn over." She picked up one end. "Lightweight. This beauty will portage easily." She started to pull it across the cement. "Crash, grab your end. We'll launch her."

"Hold it! Never drag a folboat. You'll scratch the bottom, maybe rip it. Gently. Lift it. Okay, good."

We carried our sleek prize to the launching ramp, waded alongside a flotilla of rowboats, and tied her to a piling. We could christen her later—with a Pepsi. We hurried back to erect the other kayaks. Everyone helped except June, who bumbled around in our way. Her scrawny wrists buckled as she wrestled the keel, her muscleless forearms wilted under the stress of vinyl. Her hands, too weak to spring the hasps, fluttered along poles like butterflies. Her breath gave out as she tried—for ten minutes—to tug a hull into position. Her glasses slipped off as she strained over a crossframe. Only her gray eyes seemed calm, strong. I glanced at them while she tied on her life jacket. "This little boat loves you, Crash," she said. "You really know how to put it together." She paused. "I'm sorry about what I said in the car."

"Pick up your half, puny, and help me lug it to the water." I felt another poem coming on, and I didn't want to listen. She lifted a boat end and staggered across the grass and down the ramp—but held on.

In the stern of folboat #1 Rollie sat balancing a double-bladed paddle. Her orange life jacket fit snugly over her sleeveless sweatshirt. I noted our gear, stowed under the front and rear decks. Everything shipshape. "All aboard, Crash, Lalla. Go kiss your mommie good-bye, June baby. This is it."

June trekked back to the car, where her mother had waited the entire hot hour. We saw her pat June's mouse-brown bangs into place and give her a handkerchief and a small purse. "I can't believe it," exclaimed Rollie. "Where does Mrs. Idiot think we're paddling to? A sad movie? A funeral? Who needs a hankie?"

"June can spend that money at Miami Beach. We'll take a slight detour across the 'Glades to the Eden Roc gift shoppe," said Lalla from her loungy space between us. "Who is Mrs. R. waving at? Beckoning? Must be you, Crash."

"Oh brother! What now?" I climbed out of the bow. "Save my seat, you guys." I ran the few yards to the driver's side. "What now, Mrs. Regan?"

She appeared downcast. She held June's hand through the window. She started to speak, but broke off and hunched over the steering wheel. She blew her nose. Water drops fell on the gearshift. Tears—my worst thing. Worse than—worse than poetry.

"Oh, Crash dear," she finally croaked. "I wanted to say—I wanted to ask you. Watch over my frail girl." She wept more while I roamed my eyes in embarrassment. "June's not an experienced boater like you." Sob. With my left foot I nudged a coconut under the car. So what else is new? "She can scarcely swim." Sob. I cinched my belt another notch and shook my canteen. So take her home, stupinsky. "She may need you in case—" Sob.

I heard Rollie hollering, "Cast off. Move it." I wanted to move. I felt weird. I wanted to stomp away from the weeper but seemed rooted in the grassy parking lot. To end this tearfest I finally blurted out, "I will, Mrs. Regan. I'll do it. I promise. Whatever she needs . . ."

"And I'll take care of Crash," June whispered, letting go of her mother's hand. "Good-bye for now."

Rollie shouted, "That baby needs a rattle, not a paddle," as we watched June lift herself awkwardly into #3 folboat. She nearly swamped it.

"Maybe a rain hat instead of that goofy sun visor," I said, noticing clouds ahead. We steered north on the wilderness waterway.

JUNE 2nd

A.M.

But it didn't rain Monday. And now Tuesday's rising sun riddled our canvas walls, throwing tan light on my sleeping tent mates. I stretched to see Rollie's watch, laid on a neat heap of sneakers, binoculars, bowie knife, and compass. Six A.M. Time to glide away from our Whitewater Bay campsight. I sat up, listening for morning sounds. Nothing but bird racket and a far-away motorboat. I sniffed for frying Spam. Nothing but Lalla's hair spray and talcum powder. She snored daintily from her air mattress. I whispered, "Welcome to the wilderness, you pink plastic hair rollers," to her head, which was propped on an unused sleeping bag. I scrunched back down. Another hot day coming at us for sure, but we'll stroke like fiends anyway.

We'd made great time so far. In the nine hours' sunlight left after our instructions we raced up Buttonwood Canal, across Coot Bay, through narrow Tarpon Creek, and into huge Whitewater Bay. All in a rush. All together, thanks to Miss Konecky, who paddled for two with June. Now our

four folboats lay prow to prow on the sandy beach
we'd found for camping. Through mosquito netting I could see old #1, with its wreath of sea-grape
leaves tied to the crossframes. Lalla had scanned
passing banks for orchids or moonvine to weave
into a bow crown for the christening. No luck.
"Plain leaves aren't grand enough for this beauty.
No blossoms, no name," said Rollie. So #1 remained nameless.

Wichity . . . wichity . . . wichy.

Kidick . . . kidick . . . kidick.

Oong-ka-choonk

Kew . . . kew . . . kew.

Birds summoned, still the only signs of life in
camp. Everyone was beat after yesterday's paddle.
I zipped stealthily out of our tent, pulled on shorts
and tank top, and made for a quickie swim. At the
waterline I noticed footprints—a small human,
headed east. I followed, trying to step into the same
feet. My spreadier instep wiped out track for track.
My stride, much longer, broke ahead and romped
right up to a sand sculpture with some words
printed underneath:

I will be earth you be the flower
You have found my root you are the rain
I will be boat and you the rower
You rock you toss me you are the sea

The pile of wet sand appeared to be a face, up-
turned shell nose, shell eyes turned inward. Bird-

feather bangs fringed a head that was outlined with bottleglass. Pebble ears seemed to be listening.

"June's up. Beware" came a voice from the water. I turned to see her wading in the shallow bay. I ignored her. She lay in a dead man's float.

"Better look out. You can't swim," I called eventually, watching her sink, thrash, sink, thrash in two feet of water. "I won't save you this early in the trip." Or at all, you creep. If Rollie were here we'd give you a good scare. Duck you and that. I dragged my toes through the sand face. I pushed the eyes farther inward. I scuffed out the cheeks. "You're polluting the beach with your pictures and poetry."

"Those lines aren't mine," she said quietly, ashore now at my elbow. "They're written by a genuine poet."

"Emily Bloomers?" I rubbed out "boat" and "rower." I stepped on "sea."

"No, a *living* poet, one we studied last winter in English."

"No such thing as a live poet. They're all dead. Brokenhearted. They've dropped like stones from love attacks. They've croaked on their own mushy words."

"You were in class the day we read her. I remember you threw your book out the window and got sent to the office."

"*HER?*"

"The poet. 'You rock you toss me.'"

"No thanks. I'm going back for breakfast and real life."

A small wave, the first of our journey, wiped out the sand writing. Tide must be turning. I plunged in and swam along the shoreline until toast and hash smells met me, then Lalla shaking her slinky shirt. She called, "Crash, we're having a fashion show with breakfast, so get dressed up—your fancy two-toned windbreaker, your reversible hood."

"I'm wearing what I have on. I'll dry while I'm eating." I felt tempery after my encounter on the beach. I hailed Rollie at the campstove. "Pile up my plate." I struck our tent and hauled it and our ground sheets to the boat. Then I flopped down in last night's campfire circle and ate with the gang.

"Miss Janet Grant, wearing a dazzling white pullover, trala." Our cheerful, lumpy Janet rose, chewing and giggling. "Baggy blue shorts and shocking-pink sunburn round out her traditional color scheme. She's a flag." Lalla stopped announcing and saluted.

"I hurt," giggled Janet.

"Use lots of suntan oil today, kids," warned Miss Konecky. "Especially with this breeze coming up. Windburn adds to pain."

Lalla pushed on with the fashion show. "Miss Grace C. Tallerico of Coral Gables' famous horsey family, starring in her next-to-best bathing suit, gummy brown, piped with mud."

"Wear a shirt, too, G.C., or you'll be cooked alive." Miss Konecky rose next and struck a model's pose.

"Miss Edie Konecky, veteran science teacher at Dade Jr. and gifted outdoorswoman, brings us the fashion Everglades look." Miss K. bowed. "Note first her stylish bush jacket, long-sleeved for protection against chiggers and ticks. It's smashing. Also windproof, water repellent, absolutely covered with huge patch pockets . . ."

Rollie cut in. "You showed some smarts with those pockets, Miss Konecky. You can stash all your emergency supplies in them. Have rope handy, matches, flashlight . . ."

"From skipper-blue jacket to putty-brown pants, frontier-style with tapered legs and slash pockets. Rugged twill. Neat." Lalla caught her breath, nodding at Miss Konecky's hat. "The wide-brimmed straw planter's hat protecting her fine gray hair is hand-woven. How's that for shade? Wear your own umbrella."

"Better than a dumb sun visor," I said to June, who had finally showed up for breakfast.

"Notice Miss Konecky's feet in her canvas Topsiders. These aren't your ordinary tennis shoes! No indeed! Their rubber outsoles have anti-skid tread. They're strong, supple—and groovy."

"And I'm hot as a pistol in all this fashion. Let's hope for a cooling shower by noon." Miss Konecky unbuttoned her bush jacket a few inches and blew on herself. "Now up stakes, girls, and we'll be off. Get cracking or I'll have to use the lash." She swung a tent rope around her head.

I was regaining my good spirits, so dragged Rollie alongside me and said, "Hold on, you guys. MacMaster and Adams, those twin demons of style, wish to present each other." I threw a thumb at

Rollie. "On my left you will observe the well-got-up MacMaster in Lee denim cutoffs and sticky gym socks. Notice her color-coordinated bandaids. Plus, the rubber band that holds her ponytail matches her scabby knees."

Rollie stood tall and bellowed, "I can lick any ranger—or model—in the house." We laughed and began picking up the breakfast leftovers. "Just a minute," she continued. "On my right you will observe the wild child, moody Adams. Temperamental as a grizzly. Reckless as a hawk. Tough as a crocodile heart. Willful. Just like me, in fact. Except shorter." She punched me in the ribs. "She wears her usual seedy hand-me-downs. How about her shorts, you guys? Half cloth, half holes. And these sandals? Something like a hog's dinner, right?" She pulled my braids. "Her yellow pigtails come straight out of a comic strip." She thumped me hard. "Up and at 'em, Crash. Set the old jaw in your I-dare-you look!"

"You're a double-feature nightmare of fashion," said Lalla, shaking her curls at us both. "But you sure can lift. Tote all this junk to Number One and let's blow."

Whitewater Bay soon sloshed against our nameless folboat. We'd been the last to cast off, and remained well behind the others. Lalla paddled half-heartedly in the bow. I steered dreamily from the stern. Too much breakfast or something. Rollie lay with Lalla's radio on her ear, waiting for a weather report. I sang "Got to Find My Corner of the Sky" with the Jackson Five.

"How about that for a song?" I shouted to anyone, for June's boat had disappeared ahead. "I go for those words even if they rhyme."

"The other boats slipped between the islands coming up," Lalla said. "June's not near enough to browbeat."

"Let's put a move on them. Pull harder, Lalla. Fling your back into it." Rollie tried to paddle with her feet but couldn't reach. We sprinted through the aquamarine water before Lalla complained of the heat and pooped out in a narrow pass thick with jumping fish. Rollie sat up and said, "Midway Keys, Midway Pass. I remember this scene from last year. Dad reeled in a mangrove snapper right near that channel marker. Bay's choppier today."

I wound the boat sharply west, then north until we sighted our companions about five hundred yards northwest. "The radio! Up the sound! Me and Michael will do a duet while I overtake Miss Konecky and Junie." I joined him in the last verse of "Ben." I thought about June—we'd all turned her away.

But then I pooped out of breath trying to sing and catch up. "That song could wipe your heart out if you'd let it," I panted.

Rollie grouched, "Even if they rhyme? Come on, Lalla. Fall in with Crash. She can't do all the work." She lay back down and counted beats for us to stroke by. "I'll be coxswain. One. Two. One two. Onetwoonetwo. Faster! Oh, never mind. Switch places with me, Lalla. I'll put us out in front." It was Rollie's turn for a hedgehog mood.

I said, "We'll land somewhere. You aren't supposed to change positions while we're afloat." I searched ahead for a sandy key. Every island seemed covered with mangrove trees right down to the waterline. Regular thickets. "No beaches in view. Nowhere to land. Can you wait a—"

Rollie slid into the front seat as Lalla inched out. The kayak tipped left, then righted itself immediately. "What did I tell you, scaredy! These beauties are turn-over proof. Great boats. Let's move it, Crash. Let's take off our life jackets so our arms are freer." We did.

We scudded along now. We didn't wilt in the humidity, which must have been around 80 percent. Rollie's wide nape glistened with sweat. Her bodyshirt began to ooze moisture as she lashed into ripples and the occasional swells from passing motorboats. My own eyes stung with salt water trickling from my forehead, but I managed to see the channel markers and steer our course. I could feel Rollie begin to unfrown as we gained on the others. She loosened up. Her ponytail bobbled in paddling rhythm. Her strong shoulders let down a little. She stopped counting under her breath. She glanced at her watch and said, "Flip on WINK. Time for the weather."

Static filled the steamy air along with tambourines, pianos, and drums. Over them came a male voice mingled with Dionne Warwick's: "Gathering force . . . What the world needs now . . . erratic pattern on the satellite picture . . . is love . . .

squall line . . . sweet love . . . Haiti's north . . . No, not just for some . . . warning . . . But for everyone . . . tidal waters . . . everyone . . . Aretha."

Rollie asked, "Can't you get it clearer?"

"That's not Aretha Franklin. It's Dionne." Lalla fussed with the dial until a clear, deep voice said, "Temperature—ninety-two degrees. Widely scattered showers in P.M. High tide today at eleven A.M. Low at five-eighteen P.M."

Right then we drew alongside folboat #3. I gave June a last fierce squint. Her ugly terry-cloth shirt looked as if she'd dried an ocean with it. "Did you work up that sweat helping Miss K. or writing poetry?" I asked, feathering another pint of water on her as we swooshed by.

"I don't write anymore," she said to our wake.

"What's the weather report, girls? No, don't tell me. Hot, impossibly hot," Miss Konecky called. "We're watching for Cormorant Pass. Rollie, get out there and lead. You've been through it. Watch for Marker Forty at the entrance. Keep left of it."

"I'll find the way, don't you worry," Rollie shouted backward, and to us she said, "No big deal. The channel markers wind around those islands like a trail of Gretel's breadcrumbs. Except birds can't eat steel marking buoys."

For several miles we tried to outrace cheetahs. Our paddles bit the bay and lifted ripples past the hull in precise, furious strokes. We pulled together like a couple of champs. Not counting. Not talking except for Rollie's "Good girl" to me and "Way to go" when we shot past folboat #4. Lalla fooled around with the radio until she happened onto a country-and-western station. "Better than static," she decided as we swooped down on G.C. and Janet in #2. We drew even.

"We're going thataway," Rollie said, tilting her head toward a maze of keys in the distant north-west. Sweat dripped from her chin. We both sat in puddles of our own saltwater and Whitewater Bay drippings.

"What's your hurry? Let's play some wild animal ball while the others catch up." G.C. changed her paddle to one hand and blooped a flabby rubber ball into #1. Lalla tried to toss it back into Janet's waving hat but overthrew as we dashed by their prow. Janet giggled.

Rollie couldn't resist a ball game. "Around, Crash. Cut right. Back for that ball." We backpaddled left until she reached the half-sinking blob. She snatched it, squeezed it out, flung it accurately into #2—all in one motion. "Dead center. Score one for us."

"No, Rollie. The idea is to keep the ball in the air. Volley it. Don't try to drop it between Janet and me." G.C. lobbed a perfect shot back at me.

"Who says!" I said. I socked the ball hard with my paddle. It soared toward mangroves' out-stretched arms, landing in a tangle of low branches.

G.C. turned her boat sharply toward the island. We came about, too, and matched #2 stroke for stroke. We battled up to the muddy bank. "I'm tallest. I can reach the ball," said Rollie when we'd brought our prow into the slime. "Hold 'er steady, Crash. I won't have to get out at all. I'll stand on my seat. I'll . . . I'll . . . Uffff."

Rollie went overboard, tipping us dangerously starboard. She disappeared right under. I rammed my paddle deep in mud. I held on, making #1 fast to the bank. Lalla came to life, dropped her radio, tossed a life jacket when Rollie's head broke water. "I don't need that stupid thing. It's only about four feet deep here. I'm standing up now, toes thick in muck. Ech." A large bird squawked by Rollie's ear. Minnows jumped near the stern as I tried to wrench my paddle free and boost us toward Rollie. "Steady where you are, Crash. It'll be easier for me to walk there."

But not so easy. She could hardly pick her feet up from the slimy baybottom. She came toward us in clompy Frankenstein moves, not the swift Rollie we knew. We waited under a canopy of mangroves. We slapped gnats and shrieked to our pal.

"Swamp wader."

"Sluck, sluck. Lift those iron feet."

"Slow-motion MacMaster, star of Everglades' accidents."

"You're all scuzzy, Rollie. Rinse off before you climb in next to me. You'll muss up my new shorts." Lalla withdrew her hand of help. "I'll throw you a washcloth if you want. And soap." Rollie splashed a second, then started to hoist herself aboard. I drove the paddle to its blade top in mud to keep from capsizing. Steady. Steady.

Then. A real shriek. A warning stained the air. "Snake on that limb! Snake. Snake!" Janet's voice, a giggle no longer.

She pointed directly above Lalla's head. Instantly we all looked up and searched the tangled branches. Streaky sunlight caught my eyes. I blinked. I saw our striped ball, just where I'd thrown it ten minutes ago. I saw vines snaking around fatter vines. I saw leaves trembling slightly in the breeze. I saw a limp licorice stick twisting slowly among twigs. My eyes stuttered. My brain winced, but I sat absolutely still. We all sat except Rollie, who stood alongside. Very quiet for Rollie. She whispered, "There's your water moccasin, Crash."

The licorishy snake poked his flat nose down. Down a little more as he held the limb with the other nine-tenths of himself. Down toward #1. I couldn't see a fang. Could he see us? Could he count our bodies and plan to bite us three before Rollie wrung his neck? Could he hear my thumping heart? Would he strike for it first? Did he smell the scratched-bloody midge bites on my neck? Does he love red corpuscles? Would he go for the jugular? I watched his forked tongue flick over his nostrils. He opened his mouth, and I saw his nickname—cottonmouth. White lips. White gums. Ivory fangs. A sizzling hiss. His hideous elongated eyes said, "Death."

"He means business," Rollie whispered.

We waited motionless in the bowered green light. Wavelets lazed toward the bank and slushed mangrove roots. The 'Glades seemed to sigh at our fear. Janet was a terrified lump in #2's bow. G.C. never looked away from the limb. Rollie's freckled forehead gushed sweat. Lalla seemed to be sobbing noiselessly, her curls wilting before my eyes. Her Maybelline ran black. She clutched a towel and cake of soap, minutes before offered to Rollie. Would a good warm bath soothe a pit viper? We'd soon find out, for the moccasin dropped himself into the tropical bay, a few feet from Rollie.

He coiled and struck from the surface of the water. He struck aggressively at the vinyl hull. He struck at the blade of Lalla's paddle, which dangled in the shallows. He vibrated his tail against bay-water, feinted left, struck right at Rollie mired in his path. His paired fangs passed within inches of her hand holding the life jacket. A miss! His thin mouth broke into a smile, a sneer, as he backed, recoiled, and struck again. But Rollie was ready now. She held her jacket over her stomach—his target. His fangs burst through the orange canvas covering and into the stuffing like two small swords. Yet Rollie didn't fade. She knew about thickness. She stuck fast and watched him withdraw from the fluff, taking a bit of nylon from the jacket's innards.

He struck again. More fluff. He struck again. Rollie didn't waver. She watched until his head turned, swung away from her body. His midlength followed slowly. His tail kept dipping below the surface in rapid beats as he swam shoreward, left, then under.

"He can strike underwater," Rollie muttered

while the slender, three-foot shadow slithered deeper, deeper, like a submarine avoiding depth charges. If we only had some TNT. Or a gun. Or a—

"Rollie, your bowie knife! On your belt. Underwater. Reach for it. Pull it out. Make ready," I stranglescreamed.

"Never mind that," said Rollie calmly. "Just let me get into the boat before that killer makes a pass at my ankles. He can bite through muck." She began tugging her feet from the baybottom. "Put your weight against the port side, both of you. I'll climb in opposite, for balance."

The boat rocked, but not much, as Rollie lifted and threw herself aboard. She lay a long minute sucking air. Lalla's sobs ebbed to a snivel. I twisted in my seat and circled the boat with my eyes, hunting the submerged moccasin. G.C. and Janet sat mute, snakescared, not even swatting at the swarm of furious gnats divebombing them. To buck us up I finally said, "Old Fang must have fallen in love with our beachball, guarding it that way. Or else he's a vacationing soccer goalie. Leave it in that tree for him." I wrestled my paddle from the gumbo bank and eased us backward. "Come on, Number Two, let's whip water."

Rollie said, "Probably a female, guarding her brood. Anyway, cottonmouths are supposed to be unpredictable, undependable. Here we had a biter. Last one I saw just lay around on the bank as we passed in Dad's motorboat." She sat up and tied on her life jacket. "Right here's where he struck," she said, fingering six puncture marks. "They're still wet with poison. Or rain."

I noticed then the sprinkles. Little more than a mist. It cooled us. It soothed us. "I hope it washes off that hip-high chocolate pudding on you, Rollie, before you slop it all over our bedding," Lalla said, revived and paddling.

We left G.C.'s ball, the mangrove island, our fear behind. But not the drizzle. It clung to us like freshwater sweat. It watered our necks bent low in steady stroking. No one seemed to care. We headed toward Cormorant Pass with misted eyes alert for Marker 40, the entrance buoy. Whitewater Bay chopped by, whitecaps raised in the mounting breeze.

"Windier!" shouted G.C. from their course off our stern.

"Harder to steer," panted Janet.

"My hair's ruined," said Lalla, never missing a stroke in the rain. "The crease has gone out of my pants."

Rollie said, "I needed a shower," and rubbed at her muddy legs with a ground sheet. She began singing, "Yo ho heave ho," to the tune of "Song of the Volga Boatmen." "Pull together, pull together, yo ho heave ho. I always sing in the shower. Heave ho. Heave. Heave."

"Thar she blows—Buoy Forty!" I let out a "yippie!" "Coming up on our left!"

"On our port side," Rollie corrected me, her voice as mocky as usual. That cottonmouth—the waves—the rain—nothing put Rollie down! No way.

"You're unbitable, Rollie pal," I answered her mock.

Zap by the buoy and into Cormorant Pass. Zap through this narrow aisle between two rows of small islands. Zap among mangrove roots, turtles, tall blue wading birds, diving brown-crested birds that surface with billsful of fish. Zap past Markers 42 and 44 on our right, 45 on our left. Zapping west, northwest, north past Marker 48. Billowy thunderclouds gather ahead. Rollie says, "I hope we aren't zapped by lightning bolts just as we catch up with lunch. Look there now."

She waved her mangy washcloth at a key—little more than sand bar—coming up square ahead. On it two folboats crowded two figures trying to huddle under a single rain parka. Miss Konecky stooped over a campstove, lighting match after match. June stood alone beneath the island's only tree, a small white mangrove. Oyster Bay slapped her frumpy maroon shoes.

"What kept you? I've been waiting," she seemed to say. But didn't.

JUNE 2nd

"MacMaster hung in there, eyeball to eyeball with that murderer."

"Then what?"

"She used her life jacket as a sort of matador cape. The snake saw orange. She twirled him into a fury. He sprang." I cocked two fangfingers and shot them sharply toward Mary Ann. She almost choked on her beans.

"Oh, Crash. I can't handle it," she said.

"What happened next?" asked Bette, edging closer to hear better over the frequent thunder.

"He sprang again. About eighty-three times. Show them the teethbites, Rollie." I gave my hero a friendly jostle.

Rollie smoothened her sodden life jacket. "Here, right here. But . . . uh, uh—don't touch. You might get his poison into an open cut or hangnail. Then you're goners."

Bette inspected the damage, looked up at me, and said "Oh, come on, Crash—eighty-three times? There's only six dinky punctures near the straps. That's all. Where are the rest? Why aren't these gashes?" She poked her fork toward the life jacket. "Water moccasins sport needle-thin fangs. Not meat cleavers, dope. Plus, that fellow had pinpoint accuracy. He struck the exact same hole almost every time." I scooped up my share of beans, poured rainy mustard over them, and bragged with a mouthful. "Yeah, then that coward stuck his tail between his coils and slunk away underwater. A true boob. He said 'Uncle.' Bubbles came to the surface. Rollie could have made jelly out of him if she'd wanted."

Janet giggled nervously. G.C. sneezed, muttering something about a cloudburst. June drew nearer and examined the bites. She seemed satisfied with our exaggerated tale. "You're courageous, Rollie," she whispered at length.

Rollie licked her lips, then stuffed down a fistful of cornbread. She chewed, saying, "Oh, definitely, Junie. I mostly get bored being so brave all the time." She threw back her head and drank rain. I threw back mine to admire her.

I said, "Why not immortalize her in an epic, poet? Maybe Rollie-Ticky-Tavi, Florida's answer to the mongoose. Stalwart cobra killer. Clout 'em in the hood . . ."

"I can't write poems anymore . . ."

"Nonsense. Cobras we don't have in the Everglades," shouted Miss Konecky over a thunder rumble. "Only their cousins, the coral snakes. Gather round for afternoon instructions. Crash. Rollie. Break out those tarpaulins of yours. We'll rig a lean-to so my maps won't be ruined."

With our one pitiful tree and a tent pole for uprights, a driftwood branch for crosspole, muddy rubber for cover, we fashioned a sloppy shelter just big enough for four. Each folboat captain crept near the map, now spread on a grub box. G.C., Bette, Rollie listened, watching as Miss Konecky pointed her pencil. I crouched outside, close enough to see and hear. June hung around, too.

"We're making excellent time, despite this weather. You're better boaters than those Miami University girls I brought up the waterway during Easter vacation."

"Naturally," said Rollie. "The younger the tougher."

"I figure we've traveled eighteen miles from Flamingo to our lunch site here." Miss K. tapped her pencil on the map. "Here, just south of Shark Cutoff."

"Leaving us eighty-two miles to paddle. Simple." Rollie began to back out of the lean-to. "I've covered the whole hundred miles in one day—in my dad's big powerboat, of course."

"Girls, when the rain lets up we can slow down, dawdle if we wish. We'll study the natural life. We'll still arrive at Everglades City ranger station by Sunday afternoon."

Under her breath June said, "My mother will meet us there." I said, "Big deal." Rollie, at my elbow now, said, "The rain's washed our dishes. Pack 'em up and let's kiss off this quicksandy bar." Miss Konecky called, "Come back, Rollie, and take note of our course. We're entering Little Shark

River here, then almost due north into Shark River to Tarpon Bay. We'll overnight at Canepatch Camp."

Rollie paid no attention. She filled her mouth with a fingergob of peanut butter and ransacked the others' food supplies for dessert. She shouted, "Cookies. Cookies. My kingdom for a cookie." Her long tanned legs did the chocolate-chip stomp when she lit onto her favorites in June's little-old-lady suitcase. "Got any more of these, poet, hidden down under your sun bonnets?" She rooted around in clothes, gave up, sat down in the shallows, and tossed pebbles at my sandals. June was in the shelter now and didn't answer.

"I want us to stick together this afternoon, girls. Close as a wolf pack. Captains, take the stern and hold your crafts on course. No more spills. Keep your weight low in the boat. Don't try to stand up. Bowmen will set the paddle rhythm, watch for underwater obstacles, other boats, or anything else that might come our way."

"Who'd be out in this rain but us gusty ecology types?" Rollie shouted, bailing #1 and easing it into Oyster Bay.

Lalla moaned, "It's my turn to relax. Okay, Rollie? Even a charter member of Nature, Inc., gets frazzled every so often."

"Me too. I feel like I've been rowing a coal barge all morning," Janet said, unrevived by our drenched lunch. She seemed too tired even to giggle. She scowled some.

Miss Konecky rolled up the maps and came out

of the lean-to. "Paddle with your back, not just your forearms. Work with your whole trunk. In this crosswind you'll need additional muscle voltage to stay on course." She stuck a licked finger up to test the wind. A second later she laughed at her streaming hand, lowering it to gather the tarps. "Janet, why don't you exchange places with June. Join me in Number Three. I'll paddle harder. Let you rest."

"G.C., you've lost your partner and gained a boob," said Rollie, as we varoooooomed past #2 and into the Little Shark.

Lalla murmured, "Couldn't you lay off June?" from her snoozing position. She opened an eye, adding, "If only she wouldn't wear those tacky beige pedal pushers. Must have been her mother's. Next it'll be knickers!"

We all paddled savagely, as if to escape the rain. Rollie, intent on maintaining her usual lead, alternated praise and abuse to speed me up. "Gorgeous stroke, Adams. Nice. Nice. Cuff those ripples. More. More, Custardhead! No, don't slap. Smoother. Smooth now, Crashbuddy. Waytogo. No meandering. Prod those swirls. Easy. Easy. Ease off, stupid. Backwater. Attagirl. Ohoh, Number Three's gaining. Swat water, Adams. A lot of Donner and Blitzen now. Show me your best. Show me. That's it. That's exactly it. We'll dust them off, Swifty. Dig into this motorboat wake coming up. You're a tiger. Hit it. Hit it. Don't sweat about our shimmy. No sweat. Drive. Drive. No time to be a pussycat. Attagirl. Attagirl."

Two small outboards putted past, heading downstream. A fisherman waved at us with one hand, bailed with the other. "Think it's gonna rain, honey?" another called back over his fading motor.

"Got any other original lines, buster?" answered Rollie. "You and your one-twentieth-horsepower engine. You should be stroking upriver like us kids." To me she said, "Hammer that water. Gunboat Island coming up to the right. Watch those mangrove roots."

Soon we whipped our Kayak into Shark River, slowed, grabbed breath, waited for the slugs. Wildflowers colored our prow, caught there from low-hanging vines we'd slashed in our haste. "Still no air plants," Rollie said. "I'm holding out for a mule-ear or green-fly orchid before we christen our rain barrel here." She thwacked vinyl with her cup and kept on bailing.

"Number Two's caught some flowers, Rollie, if you'd like these for your ceremony." G.C. hove alongside, pointing to purple blossoms.

"Floating hearts," said June. "They're yours if you want. *Nymphoides cordata*."

"Great pack we've been, straggled along the river like lone wolves!" Miss Konecky blew her whistle. It sounded sore about something. "I really must insist we remain together. Rollie, keep your boat in line behind me. I want to feel Crash breathing on my neck but not blowing by." We set out again. "I mean it. Behind me. Let Number Two take the lead. You stay behind. Mind me."

Lalla woke to ask if we'd see sharks cruising

Shark River. Rollie said, "Not this far inland. Only where it empties into the Gulf—at Ponce de Leon Bay. A few hammerheads maybe. Dad caught one there last summer. Now, crocodiles—they're all around here. Everywhere." She could really soothe a guy.

"Girls, did you notice that mangrove forest on either side of the Little Shark, just as we came through the cutoff? Some of those trees are fifty feet tall." Miss Konecky began a three-mile lecture when the thunder died away. The crews paddled three abreast to stay in earshot. Number One sidled up behind, following orders. "Hurricane Donna tore tops off the eighty-footers back in nineteen sixty. You were still babies."

"I remember old Donna. One-hundred-and-forty-mile-an-hour winds. Took the roof off our cottage down in the Keys."

I said, "You must have watched from your bassinette, Rollie. You aren't that much older than us."

"Mangroves come back strong, though. Just look at this wilderness of roots bristling from the mud. Impossible to wade ashore here. And their branches —so thick they obliterate the sky." Miss Konecky pointed her paddle. She pointed at a wedge of woodstorks flapping above the mangroves, at dragonflies zinging among the glossy green leaves. She pointed above at an egret rookery, below at the nest of a round-tailed muskrat in the roots. She pointed out a bald eagle's nest—big, sloppy pie in dead limbs. She pointed out a string of white ibis, a family of raccoons, a school of mosquitofish. She pointed out a lone anhinga, perched, drying his wings overhead. She pointed from turtles to lizards to green tree frogs. She pointed ahead to our sharp right turn into Tarpon Bay, to marsh grass along its banks, to a houseboat chugging our way. She pointed behind her head at the sun, rambling out from clouds that moved north. I felt it before I saw the reflection in the Bay. "Sun's drying my bush jacket."

"Hope it unwrinkles my headband," said Lalla, sleepily rising to greet the houseboaters.

A little girl hollered from the deck, "We're going home. We're all wet." Her mother called, "Aretha's making a mess of things," as she hung clothes to dry on a sagging line.

"I don't see any diapers," I said.

"We're soaked, too, but we'll dry out before we get to camp," called Rollie boisterously to the putt-putt. I felt our stern jiggling like crazy, and turned to find Rollie sort of tangoing in her seat. She sang, "Ham for dinner. Yams and ham. Hurray."

I sang, "You're a ham, Rollie. I'll take a bite out of you as an hors d'oeuvre." I ground my teeth. I drank Cherry Smash from my canteen. "Stop dancing or you'll pitch us overboard."

For an hour or more we all stuck together crossing Tarpon Bay. We were silent except for an occasional outburst from sleep-talking Lalla. "Oh, my poor droopy socks," she said once, and "Must shave my legs," and "Sweating gives me pimples."

At the northeast corner of the bay we slipped

into a skinny passageway. "Avocado Creek, girls. We can slack off without worry. We'll arrive at Canepatch before dark."

"A neat camp, too. Wait'll you pick bananas right beside your tents. Wild limes. Even papayas. And sugarcane to suck." Rollie was up on her knees now, paddling Indian-style. We glided alongside Miss Konecky. Rollie's turn to lecture. "Seminoles used to live around here. Calusas before them. You can still find their garbage dumps—shell tools, animal bones, human teeth, and stuff. They ate alligators. Ugh. Not exactly your premier ham dinners. Lots of feasting places along this creek, now the mangroves thin out." She pointed her paddle Konecky-style.

We had edged well past #3 when Miss Konecky reined us with a question. "Seen any snakes this afternoon, Crash? Rollie? Lalla? Flat-tailed water snakes can be found on the waterway. Also the banded water snake. Both harmless and really quite lovely. Maybe we'll run into an Everglades rat snake at the campground. He's non-poisonous, of course. Beautifully yellow and agile."

A chorus of "I hope nots" slammed that comment, but G.C. kept the subject going with "Is it true that if you kill a venomous snake the mate will seek revenge? You know, come after you and kill you back?"

Lalla shot up from her sleep. "You mean the snake wife will chase her husband's slayer? Lay in wait? Bite? That sort of thing? How does she? . . .

Oh, June! We're in big trouble just because your mother ran over . . ." She jerked up her limp socks for protection.

I curled my fingerfangs again, lunged them around in mid-air, and said, "Our pygmy rattler's wife awaits us at the old tenting grounds. Watch your ankles."

"Silly children. You've been reading snake fairy tales, not facts about reptiles. G.C., June, make ready to tie up at the dock just ahead. The rest of you girls follow Number Two. Easy. Steady. Steady there. There." The dock gave a soft, yielding thump. We'd arrived.

"Anyway, that pygmy probably wasn't even married," Rollie said to reassure our frightened pals.

The smell of bananas perfumed Canepatch Camp, luring us from duties. I started to stake down our tent but instead found myself sauntering around in the dense undergrowth, hunting wild sugarcane. Vines tangled around my neck; Spanish bayonet caught my ragbaggy shorts. In the heavy, darkening air, mosquitoes made loop-the-loops, preparing for their suppers of blood—ours. I swatted a dozen. I worked up a sweat waving my arms to keep them at bay. My own heat rose to tempt them further. Better go back for long sleeves and mosquito spray. My stomach rumbled as I backtracked. I crashed out of the jungle and into our clearing, greeted there by Lalla sleepily pirouetting around the small campfire.

"Not exactly ballroom condition, this outfit. But at least I've changed. Couldn't stand myself any longer." She wore a wrinkleless pants suit. Dove gray. Monogrammed, yet. She danced with an armful of darkness, humming in time to her transistor.

"Cut it out, Lalla. Stand still and watch our meat so it doesn't burn." Rollie's voice from the tent. "Crash, get on in here and huff up the air mattresses. Let's get organized."

I took orders. I made our beds, carefully spreading the sleeping bags as pillows. We'd never need them for covers. Not in this heat. I unzipped window flaps, hoping for cross ventilation—or just any air at all. I laid out pajamas, toothbrushes, hairbrushes, everything but Lalla's curlers and movie magazines. I lit our butane lantern, went outside, hung it on a buttonwood tree, and staked down the tent fly better. I put on my jacket, Levis, and sweat socks to thwart mosquitoes, squirted myself all over with Off, flicked on my flashlight, and joined the others at the site's only table.

Elbow to elbow in the sultry night, we ate greedily, wordlessly. Janet had made grits, Miss Konecky cathead biscuits in her portable oven. There was plenty of jam, a pile of yams, thick slices from the canned Danish hams Rollie provided. "Everything but gingerbread," she said, grinning at me over the lantern.

"I brought a pie," June said softly. "I was saving it for Thursday noon—halfway through our trip."

"What kind?" Rollie pounced.

"Mama always calls it 'love pie.' Rather like mincemeat except sweeter. It's made from butter, graham crackers, molasses . . ."

"Break it out," said Rollie. "Even a love pie will rot by Thursday in this heat."

June slipped quietly from the table to the tent she shared with Miss K. She handed a flat box to Rollie. "You cut it, okay?"

Rollie kept muttering, "Too small," "dumb," and "sticky," as she divided our dessert. With a plastic spoon I fooled around the crust of my share, then tasted, then bit, then chomped through it in ten seconds. "Delicious, poet." I patted myself. "Feels like a sunset in my stomach."

"She sure can cook. Your mother. Even if she sicced a snake on us." Lalla downed her piece and added charcoal and wood to the fire, saying, "Come on, everyone . . ."

Rollie broke in. "Not enough pie for a skink's dessert. Let's pick bananas, Crash, to fill up on."

"No you don't, girls. It's too dark now to knock around this hummock."

"Even with our flashlights?"

"Or lanterns?"

"Even with a searchlight. I see little point in your courting trouble. Once you leave the fire you'll be bitten crazy by mosquitoes. You'll step on cactus. Cactus will rip those holey shorts. Snakes. You'll . . ."

"Anyway, I'm giving a dance," Lalla announced, turning up her radio to top blare.

I felt pie-mellow so didn't object. Rollie grumbled under her breath but led the way to a large cleared space—a hog pen after the rain. "Me and

Crash will dance the hoochie koochie," she called, wallowing in the mud. I tried to follow but couldn't connect with her jerks, her knee-knocking jounces. I gave up to watch the others waddling in pairs. G.C. slowly did the swineherd's jig while Janet flinched and laughed. Bette, holding Mary Ann's shirt tail, shuffled her toes under mud and said, "Oink, oink, oink, oink," in time to "My Funny Valentine." Then they locked fingers and led each other around the fringes, calling, "This gross piggie became pork chops, this gross piggie turned to ham." Miss Konecky floundered in the center of our dance hall. Then her deck shoes stayed put, her feet leaped one leap and went down for keeps. Only her partner, Lalla, remained serene, unbogged. She stood clean and swayed, even when the music ended, the news began. We all slogged on. We laughed a lot.

A lonely silhouette, still by the fire. June. She glanced from embers to dancers, humming faintly to the Florida Nightly News Round-Up. Piehigh and feeling sorry for her, I said, "Excuse me, partner. I'm cutting in on the poet. She looks shipwrecked there." I shambled over. I asked, "Wanna dance? Or rather, slop around?" I noticed then she'd changed her clothes for dinner. This time ugly seersucker. Who else but June could have found it these days? Must have been hidden in the store's broom closet.

"I'd love to, Crash." She rose and tried to waltz to the weather report. She took three steps, three more, slow. She slid right. I laughed into her hair. She slid left. I grabbed a shoulder to lead, to hold her up.

"Who's that hanging onto Mousey?" Rollie called. "Looks like sow mother and piglet. How's for a threesome?" She started our way.

"According to Miami's Hurricane Forecast Center . . ."

"Let's step it!" said Rollie by my side, ready for a threeway fling.

"Quiet, Rollie. The weather."

"Thus this first hurricane of the season, Aretha, will bypass Southern Florida if she holds to her present course."

Lalla said, "Oh, *that* Aretha." Miss Konecky said, "Turn the dial. Try to bring in WINK without static." Rollie said, "All our rain and thunder today must have been the outer edges of Aretha— the squall line." I said, "Let the bureau watch for hurricanes. I'm going to bed."

I was massively tired all at once. My back, my triceps, my wrists, even my fingernails felt stretched, sore. I shucked off my clothes and lay alone in the tent, listening to Rollie heckling June. "Only waltzer left in South Florida . . . You're gonna burn the laces off your saddle oxfords with that red-hot minuet . . . You are truly weird . . . Better just give up and read us a bedtime poem."

The radio signed off. A silence followed the cattle stampede to tents. Then June's soft voice read:

I'm Nobody! Who are you?
Are you—Nobody—too?
Then there's a pair of us!
Don't tell! they'd banish us you know!
How dreary—to be Somebody!
How public—like a Frog—
To tell your name—the livelong June—
To an admiring Bog!

Another silence. "Maybe Dickinson's trying to tell you something, Rollie," called Miss Konecky from her tent to ours.

"She's wrong," said Rollie sleepily.

I thought about Aretha. June's too soon. I started going under. The Everglades lay fast asleep. But not for long.

JUNE 3rd

DAWN

"What time is it, Rollie?"

"Uh?"

"What time is it?"

"Lemme sleep."

"Oh, anyway, it's around dawn."

Feeble light hung in the hummock. The sun seemed to be rising a ray at a time, filtered through banked clouds. Millions of clouds. Not fleecy, friendly ones, either. Instead, bundles of spiteful-looking ones skulled near treetops. Through mosquito netting I watched gray ogres drop, drop, seize branches, step into leaves, slump against trunks. "Can't tell the ground fog from clouds," I said to Rollie, hoping she'd wake to cheer me on this dirty day.

Miss Konecky's ear-busting whistle blew me from bed to our misty kitchen. "We've a long trip today, Crash. All the way over to Broad River. Better crank the stove and scramble a batch of eggs. June, shake our heavy sleepers. I'll set the table." She looked at the sky and waggled her head disapprovingly.

I mixed powdered eggs, powdered milk, water, olive oil, and salt. I lit the stove, dumped this mess into a pan, and stirred, listening to the troops waking up.

"Fog's so thick even Rollie's snake couldn't bite through it."

"Oh no. It's gonna rain again."

"What'll I wear today?"

"Your patent-leather jump suit with sequined monogram. It's fog-repellent."

"Wish I'd brought some clothes hangers."

"I smell Crash in the kitchen."

"Ah, beat it, June."

"Adams, fork over some toast. And pass the catsup. Your eggs stink. Worse than Brussels sprouts." Rollie drummed her spoon on the table and glowered. I recognized her tone of voice. Sullen. Dangerous. Like in school—in English class. She snarled, "I'm *somebody!* Who are you? / Are you somebody, too? / No way!" to her canteen as she pulled a long drink of water. She growled, "I'm *everybody!* Who the heck are you?" to June, who was scouring the frying pan with sand. She yelled, "I'm *everybody!* You're nobody! / That's a fact," at June, who by now was struggling her bulging laundry bag toward #2 folboat. "Here, let me help you with that, Miss Midnight Poet."

"That's okay. I can do . . ."

Rollie jerked the bag from June, hefted it, pulled the drawstring, and felt around in its depths. Rollie got this enraged look on her face. "You pitiful

numbskull! Why did you bring? . . ." She broke off.
She looked like she could kick a hole in June.

Everyone else was striking tents. I decided to butt
out of Rollie's scene and into the uproar of hauling
gear. I grabbed the cook pots, slunk over to #1,
stowed them, bailed dew, fiddled around with some
cushions in the bottom, and listened. To a drizzle
begin. To a sudden gust trying to harvest the wild
fruit trees. To coo-coo-coo. To folboats socking the
dock. To ker-wee. To someone crying.

Back at the fire circle June stood in tears, books
strewn around her in the sand. Rollie's voice wal-
loped her. "You're supposed to bring food, knuck-
lehead, not dictionaries. Camp supplies, not notebooks. Check this, Crash. A boxed set of love
lyrics." She pointed a sneaker at a leather heap.
"And these. Fifteen pounds of sonnets. A boodle
of trash."

I rejoined the scene. Rollie whirled the empty
laundry bag on its drawstring. I ducked. June
didn't. She got it in the ear. "Where's your snakebite pump, your painkillers, your snare wire, your
fishing hooks, your signal mirror, your emergency
rations in case you get . . ." Rollie ran out of
breath in her fury. She puffed, "Your machete,
your tea bags, your rescue flares? We may have a
hurricane on our hands some day soon. What
could you do for us then, you weepy jerk?"

June looked over at me with floodstained eyes.
They held me a long minute. Then I bent down
and salvaged a paperback. I tore pages from the
middle, handed them to June, and said, "There,

there, blow your nose on Elizabeth Barrett Browning. She deserves it." I took the bag from Rollie, squashed the other volumes back where they belonged, and hung the bag around June's neck. "Here's your albatross, Miss Ancient Mariner. Stop sniffling now. Your poems are safe."

"Girls, what's going on here? Crash? Rollie? What's the matter, June?"

June didn't answer. She lifted her firm chin. She slowly removed her heavy duffle bag collar. She blew her nose. She said, "Poems make pretty good Kleenex, among other things," and smiled.

"Rollie, I think it's time that June rode with you. In Number One. Maybe you two can patch up your differences, whatever they are. Come on, Lalla. Stroke with me for a change. I'll hold 'er steady while you paint your toenails." Miss Konecky set out in the lead.

"Well, one good thing," Rollie snarled to June about fifteen minutes down Avocado Creek. "Me and Crash will use less energy getting over to Broad River. You underweigh Lalla."

"I'll paddle my share," said June. "We can change off."

Rollie said, "Not a chance," and sulked until lunch.

JUNE 3rd

DUSK

There in the shelter of mangrove roots and branches, rain flies and flaps, ground sheets and tents, we almost forgot our showery morning, our windy afternoon, our evening spent colonizing Broad River campsite in a steady downpour. Now, dinner over, we sat together with a water bucket of popcorn, reviewing the day's miles.

"No snakes today."

"I saw two deer."

"We saw five."

"Best of all those roseate spoonbills wading the creek mouths."

"No, the swallow-tailed kite. He's rarer."

"But he's not lipstick pink like the spoonbill. I want a raincoat his very color."

"Perhaps more carmine, like a sunset over water."

"Rot, Junie. Strawberry-milkshake pink."

"How many butterflies did you count before noon, girls?"

"Not many."

"Few."

"We gave up."

"Then no one wins the prize."

"I've had it with the rain."

"My mascara ran all afternoon."

"Worst was that hairy trip through the Nightmare. I thought we'd never straighten out."

"We zigged a thousand zags."

"Plenty of snags along in there. And deadheads. I'd hate to come through in the dark."

"We'd of never made it at low tide, either. Too many logs crisscrossing the creek."

"Even worse was when I dropped my Instamatic in the Harney. I don't know what I'd do without Rollie!"

"That river's so shallow, even June could have brought it up. Plus, I'm used to going overboard."

Everyone laughed except Janet.

"Too bad your film's ruined, Bette. We could take some hilarious shots of our shantytown here."

"Lights, camera, action. The roofs fall in from an overdose of rain."

"I'll get my Polaroid," said G.C. "And some flashcubes." She didn't need to go far. We'd arranged our tents in a close-knit circle. G.C.'s two-man backpacker sagged right against the picnic table. "The lens is safe and dry," she said, lighting the group with a pop, flash. "Got it."

We left off crunching snacks and watched the birdie. Lalla lounged with her arms folded, hands stuck up her sleeves. "I don't want my ragged cuticles filmed," she said.

"You're in better shape than most of us," moaned

Mary Ann, ducking her head behind Rollie's broad back. "I'm not about to show my peeling face."

G.C. said, "One day of sun and we're totally blistered. All except June. She stayed covered." She put in another flashcube and kept shooting.

"Two stormy days and I'm wanting the whole trip done with. Honestly, I've never felt so rain-trodden." Janet hadn't giggled since breakfast. Her ear-to-ear sun blisters seemed an odd contrast to the rain splashing around us. She held a hand in front of her face to ward off G.C.'s camera.

"Take off your glasses, June. Good. Hold your head up. Now there's an untypical pose. You won't read in this one." G.C. snapped the poet sitting alone on a small camp stool. Her damp bangs lay along her pale forehead like a row of mouse tails. Her eyes were lifeless—gray emblems of a day spent in Rollie's care. Her hands, red and chappy from struggling with wet canvas, knotty ropes, lay folded around a plate of leftovers. I watched her pose for a portrait. She stiffened her back and looked direct-ly at the lens. She seemed to force a grin, a good-natured answer to insults and rain. I remembered that same smile from before. From school. As I tried to recall the moment, June's storm-weary head grew heavy and sank toward her corned beef.

She slept while Rollie mucked around the gloomy clearing, striking poses in doorways, under awnings, beside the smoldering grill. "Take me. Take me while I'm fixing this slack guy line." She thumbed her nose at the camera. "Watch how I can walk on coals. Barefoot." She kicked off her Pro Keds and strutted on the grill.

"I can't focus this thing, Rollie. You're all legs and scabs. You're up too close for a full-length picture. Get back. Over there."

Rollie stumped toward a tree that towered above the mangroves semicircling our campground. She rammed it with her shoulders, shook off raindrops, leaned against its scaly bark, stared defiantly across the distance, and said, "Snap it. Snap me. Me and this giant sequoia."

But before the click, Miss Konecky bolted her place at the table, screaming, "No, Rollie, not there. Come away from that tree." She fled across the clearing, collared Rollie, shoved her to the Broad River and in. "Lalla, where's your soap? Get it."

"What the heck?" asked Rollie, hawking up the Broad.

"Manchineel. The manchineel tree! It's poison! Fruit, leaves, sap, everything! Highly toxic." Miss Konecky jumped into the water beside Rollie and began scrubbing her with a soapy sponge from the dishpan. "You can be poisoned just standing under a manchineel during a rainstorm. Sap oozes down to give you blisters. Duck, rinse. Catch our hands, Crash. Pull."

They came out of the Broad and used up a pile of paper napkins drying off. Rollie held her arms to a lantern. "I don't see any poison. Where's the harm?"

"Manchineel toxins are water-soluble. You're fine now but believe me, you ran a risk over there. Big red blisters that ulcerate . . ."

Rollie never missed a beat. "How's about a close-up of my face, saved from ulcers by our leader."

I crowded into the picture. "Lucky MacMaster, that pug nose deserves at least one blemish besides your freckles." I tweaked my pal's nose.

"Less rain, more stars," said June, waking in time for bed. The moon swam out from behind a cloud.

"Aretha's heading away, out into the Gulf of Mexico." Miss Konecky took the radio off her ear. "We may have sun by morning, girls."

"I'd settle for Venus now," said June.

I turned in first.

JUNE 4th

VERY EARLY

Slowly a force took hold of me. An engine? Voices? Where? Where am I? I began to feel my body waking up. Motors, voices nearer. Motors dead. Whispers, rooting me out of sleep. My mind groped to understand. From some far place it struggled into listening, into hearing gruff, hushed words in the campsite. In my heart's core I knew the tone of trouble. "Lost . . . Aretha . . . Tower . . . Lostmans . . . Lostmans River Ranger Station . . . Vertical cumulus clouds development . . . Thundersqualls . . . Noticeable increase in wind velocity."

Another voice, lighter, higher, played in and out of the gruff. "Strong girls . . . Excellent paddlers . . . Making unusually good time . . . Forty miles in three days should give you some idea of their ability. They've been looking forward to this trip all spring."

I shook myself nearly awake. Miss Konecky seemed to be answering questions. "Nine of us. In high spirits, of course. Complaints? Only about the food, as usual. No we're fine, just fine. We're well equipped, as you can see. I'm sure we can make it to Lostmans River Ranger Station before noon tomorrow—I mean today. They've hardly noticed the rain."

"I noticed it," said another voice, husky with sleep.

"Fellows, this is Janet Grant, one of Nature, Inc.'s founding members. She's a specialist in small mammals."

"I hurt." An awake whine.

"She's got a brutal sunburn there," said a voice I began to recognize. I got up on my knees and looked out through the mosquito netting. A shadow in a wide-brimmed hat stood shining a powerful beam in Janet's face.

I took hold of Rollie's foot and shook it hard. "Rollie, it's rangers. That one who almost didn't let me come with you. Three other guys besides him."

Rollie said, "Uh?"

"Get up and bark at him. Something's going on out there." I shook and shook. I tousled her hair. I wrenched her ponytail around to the front and tickled her eyes with it. Finally she boomed up, ready to belt me. "Right there, belt that guy. I think he's come to wreck our trip." We were flinging on our clothes now, buttoning all wrong in the dark. I felt for a familiar zipper, only to find cold metal buttons. "These are your hip huggers, Rollie. Oh, well. I'll wear 'em till we get rid of those guys." I rolled up the too-long legs.

Then came a regular fusillade of voices. "What's happening? . . ." "Hey, shut off that light. It's right in my eyes . . ." "For crying out loud—twelve o'clock. This is getting ridiculous . . ." "Wait'll Rollie discovers your plan . . ." "Have you ever heard of beauty sleep? Mine's ruined."

While we squirmed with shirts the clearing became a thoroughfare of sleepwalking girls and milling-around rangers. Miss Konecky jumped to a picnic bench, trying to manage the night. She held her lantern aloft. She shouted, "We'll take a vote, that's fair. After all, our ecology club's democratic." No one worked up the energy to comment. Miss K. continued. "Rollie, as president, you pose the question. Crash, count raised hands."

"What question?"

"Whose hands?"

We ripped out of our tent and took a look. The mud-site bloomed with pastel campers, self-conscious in their pajamas. Three rangers, hands deep in pockets, patrolled the circle of light. Another crouched in the stern of a power launch, gunning the engine. Thunk-kapow, thunk-kapow, overwhelming Miss Konecky's explanation. "The question is," she finally sang out, "shall we strike camp now, this minute, fold our boats, and return to Flamingo with these rangers? . . ."

"Boo!"

"Never!"

"Or shall we suffer another twelve hours of rain —six tonight in the tents, six tomorrow while we paddle to Lostmans River Ranger Station?"

"Who's suffering?"

"Paddle!"

"Ride free or paddle, girls. You name it." Miss K.'s lantern sputtered out. Flashlights took over.

Rollie tipped her head to one side and pondered. Next thing she said was, "Both questions are moronic. Of course we won't go back with these guys! Why should we? And what's this about the ranger station? It lies well off the wilderness waterway—clear over to the Gulf of Mexico."

"Not far from this camp, though, Red. An easy morning's paddle with quite a few good landing places along the sand. Beaches everywhere." The compass-incident ranger motioned northwest in the dark and watched Rollie for her reaction.

"Sure, but what's the point? We're following the marked waterway, not the beaches. Tomorrow's— today's run takes us east and north, up into Rodgers River Bay, Big Lostmans Bay, to Onion Key . . ."

A hefty, bronzed ranger in war camouflage raingear elbowed through pajamas. "The point is, my dear, we've got a storm on our hands! The fringes of Aretha. We're warning all campers on the waterway to make for home the quickest way. In your case, that would mean coming along with us tonight."

"Quickest and *easiest*," said Compassking, "for you wilderness poetesses."

"Or paddle to the ranger station. You'll make it before noon today. Then we'll take you upcoast to Everglades City or back south to Flamingo. Meanwhile we'll get in touch with your folks . . ."

Rollie and this tan guy squared off. "We've been

in the squall line for two days, fellow. No problem. We're wet but warm. Plenty of grub. Tons of equipment. We're all trained first-aiders. We're no creampuffs."

"Young lady, Aretha's already shown us she's moody, unpredictable. She's cut a capricious pattern clean up from Haiti. She could strengthen, speed up, double around, and smack these 'Glades like the Okeechobee hurricane of nineteen twenty-eight. Your boating's over—right now or by noon tomorrow."

Thunk-kapow. Thunk-kapow. Chin to collarbone, the two battlers stood ready for the next punchword.

"*Hurakán,* they used to call it, kid. Named for an evil spirit. It could get you."

"Miles away, guy."

"The weather satellite . . ."

"Come down to earth."

"Small craft warnings . . ."

"Huge girls."

"Gale force . . ."

"Paddle force."

"I mind the rain. And I hurt. I want to go home now." Janet's voice separated the foes.

"Traitor!"

"She's sensible, Rollie, girls. Really, this has gone far enough. We'll be along tomorrow—today. Noon at the ranger station. Take Janet now. She'll be more comfortable there with you." Miss Konecky waved us away. "To bed again, girls."

"The cheerfulest fade first, ya phoney," Rollie

hollered, watching Janet sling her duffle to the tan one. He smiled like a winner and patted Rollie's pate. "You're all right, kid. You've been wrong—but all right. More guts than brains. You and your friend there are the only two dressed, ready for trouble. You came out of that tent like commandoes. Rope and a knife. Canteens. Shoes on. Dukes cocked."

I muttered, "You're worse than June, you blubberlump," when Janet passed me on her way to the launch. "At least the poet's sticking it out." Janet giggled for the first time that day and climbed aboard.

Where was June, anyway, all this time? I took Rollie's flotation flashlight, squirted it over the yawning campers. June, dope, there you are. Reading! What else? Reading maps like they're poems.

"Whang 'em up early, lady," came a voice from the black river. Miss Konecky answered, "I will if you'll come back when the storm passes and cut down this big manchineel. For the safety of my future tours."

"That's no manchineel. You're close, though. It's oysterwood. Same family but harmless."

I thought I heard June say, "I could have told you that."

By degrees I'd waked up. By degrees I slid back to sleep. I tossed in my sack until Rollie muttered, "Cut it out." I massaged my rain-bitten neck. I worked fingers around to my throat. I wanted a drink but couldn't reach my canteen without rousing Lalla. She'll get bags under her eyes and blame me, I thought, sucking my damp cuffs. I wished I had a lemonade. I thought about ice in a dixie cup. Fuzzy images swirled just under my eyelids. Thick-tongued but drifting, I gave in to them.

Crushed ice, slushing around in a waxy carry-out cup. A Slurpee. In this sweaty rain forest? No way. At the 7–11, across from school. Me and Mac-Master chug-a-lugging grape Slurpees at noon. "Your turn to pay, Rollie. And I won't flip you for it. You always win." Rollie laughing about her fifty-cent piece with two heads—two Kennedys. Her trick. "I can't skip English with you, either, Rollie. We've pulled that once too often. She'll catch on."

"I'll chance it," says Rollie. "She's doing poetry today. Caused me to flunk English last year. It's gonna cause me to flunk again. Only this time I'll make it up in summer school."

"Don't knock it. Without poetry I'd of never met you, remember that. You'd still be a year ahead in English, up there with the tenth-graders. Come on to class. You'll survive forty-five minutes."

"Only with a strong drink. Barkeeper, another Slurpee."

Deeper now. Three-dimensional images fading. Dream people appear. Shadows in a large room. We are among books, and ice melts down my back. Rollie sits behind me whistling, flipping pages, dropping frozen pellets under the collar of my army-surplus shirt. A Southern drawl from the blackboard: "Y'all pay 'tention, hear? Y'all just gonna love po'try, hear? Copy these words in your notebooks. You too, Rollie MacMaster, and you, Valentine. Copy." Scratchy pencils, my leaky felt tip saying, "metaphor," "simile," "rhyme scheme," "free verse," "rhythm." More drawling, droning. "List these poet'sses, hear? On another page. Mrs. Elizabeth Barrett Browning. Em'ly Dickinson. Edna St. Vincent Millay. Eleanor Wylie. List these poets in a sep'rate column."

Deeper. A dream voice chats to my brain. "The woman's a loser. A feeb . . . Crash, how can you stand that she uses your real name . . . Don't let her get away with it. Let's put a move on her, start a revolution . . ." Rollie stamping her feet toward the sharpener. Uproar around her. Books floor-ward, papers skyward. Titters from everyone but June. Shadow teacher calling roll. "Where's yur poem, Rollie? By yur own self. Due now, hear?" Rollie's completely blank page, her "Hymn to Si-lence, to Laziness, or to Your Brain, Teacher." A burst of applause from the boys. The teacher bur-rows her head in the hymn and says, "Y'all fail again, Miz MacMaster. This here is zero. Anyone can write a 'riginal poem, hear? Even you!"

Deeper even. Losing myself in the dream. I turn in blank pages, too. "I can't write about love. That's dumb. I can't write about death. I never was there. I can't do rhymes. I can't beat out my poem's rhythm on the desk. But I can stand on my hands—Rollie taught me." Me, legs, sandals in the air, up-side down by the trashbasket. Me, back at my desk,

angry and tremblish with zero for conduct, F for
the day. Me, listening to June, there near the win-
dows reading her poem to a classful of gigglers.

"Love rose early up today
Done with sleep at dawn
Love moved 'round the sunny garden . . ."

"Pulling her underpants on," shouted Rollie
with glee. "What a bunch of goo."

Deskquaking laughter now from the rows. Em-
barrassed tears from June Regan. Tossed ice cracking against the windowpanes. Paper cup's harsh
"pow" under Rollie's heel and her "Goo, 'ya hear,
y'all?" Dream sounds dragging me from dream.

"Rollie, did you say something?"

"Uh?"

An owl called through the rain noises. Lalla
mumbled, "Acne," and turned away from me in
her own dream.

I slept again, this time with a technicolor car-
toon. Woody Woodpecker voices from mouth-cov-
ered faces. Figures jerking among desks. Teacher
thumbing Rollie from the room: "To the office,
hear? The principal, hear? And take your books.
I don't want you back—ever!" Tall Rollie reeling
from blackboard to doorway, pointing a ruler at
June. "You'll get yours." Exit. That's all, folks.
Except longwinded silence, except textbooks open
again and June's recovered voice reading, reading
in a dream.

I will be earth you be the flower
You have found my root you are the rain
I will be boat and you the rower
You rock you toss me you are the sea
How be steady earth that's now a flood
The root's the oar's afloat . . .

I throw my anthology out the window and join my pal on the office bench.

That's really all. Except . . .

JUNE 4th

We wake to rain. We eat in rain. We eat rain. Rain
waters our oatmeal, Tang, and cold chocolate.
Water wars with our hands while we loosen knots,
unwrap ropes, dig stakes, pack canvas, unfasten
boats, and bail them. Rain on choppy waters. Rain
or sun blisters, mosquito bites, sore muscles. Rain
that will last through this day, washing away our
planned journey.

"What's a little rain among friends?" asked G.C.,
being cheerful in her partner's seat at breakfast.

"You should have talked Janet into staying last
night. She's half your crew, after all. She'll put a
hex on our day," Rollie growled through a mouthful of marshmallows.

Lalla twisted a stray lock of hair and gave the
clouds a vexed glance. Mary Ann sighed. "Only six
more hours of it." Bette pushed away her rain-
thinned gruel, saying, "Our trip's ruined. Oh, the
pain!" It seemed colder today. I cussed the rain.

"Girls, this rain's not all bad. We've had a very
dry winter. The 'Glades needed fresh water—for
spider lilies, balloon vines, willows. Birds starve

unless there are pools for spawning minnows. These waders depend on good fishing." She waved a wet hand toward a bird at the waterline. "Look on the bright side."

"You look," Rollie said.

"Green heron, dawn-feeding." June looked up from a book.

"We could have eaten lunch at Camp Lonesome Mound today, under the gumbo limbo. Massive trunk on that tree. Camp's way inland. There's all kinds of sea grapes around there, and nickerbeans. Plus bulrushes. I wanted to show Crash the banana patch."

"Some other time, Rollie. Maybe later on this season. I'm taking a group from Ft. Lauderdale in July or August . . ."

"Fat chance. I'll be in summer school."

Bumping of thunder led Rollie to #1. She straightened the packs, took her paddle and checked out its edges. "Nicks here and there. Splinters. Wish I had some sandpaper. Even a hairline scratch can slow us down." She watched blowing mangroves a minute. "Wind from the west. We could be in some trouble in canoes. But these kayaks here—they're safe. No dunkers this morning." She retied the line attached to the bow. "Crash, this is called the 'painter.' Funny word for a simple rope. This painter needs splicing." She took her bowie knife and began to fool around with strands of line, but just then Miss K. motioned to #2.

"Rollie, will you inspect G.C.'s weight distribution. If she's to paddle alone in the stern we'd better move her heavier gear to the front."

Rollie said, "Let's stash the crybaby there instead. She's about the same dead weight as a pup tent."

"I paddled her Tuesday," said G.C. "You other guys deserve a turn."

"Not me and Crash. We did that number yesterday."

"Rollie, why not move over with G.C.? That way you'll even up the load and . . ."

"And slow down Number One! I'm wise to your little plan." Rollie laughed, but not much. "Okay, if Number Two can take the lead today. Crash and June get to paddle the sweep boat."

"Just remember, girls. The lead boat is never passed. Sweep brings up the rear. The sweep never passes any boat. Each boat keeps the one behind it in sight, waiting if necessary." Miss K. touched her trusty whistle. "Listen for this to bring us together. Come alongside Number Three when you hear two sharp blasts. Assemble around me then for instructions. Mind—two sharp blasts."

Rollie stuck fingers between her teeth and blew shrilly. "Three big toots for Mayday. I don't need a whistle. Wheeeeeet. Wheeeeeet. Wheeeeeet. Mayday! Mayday!"

I asked, "Mayday? This is Juneday. Thursday, the fourth of June, nineteen seven . . ."

"Mayday, dummy. Don't you know? The international distress signal. Pilots holler 'Mayday' to the tower when their planes are falling down.

Skippers holler 'Mayday' to their shortwaves when their ships strike icebergs. 'Mayday, we're sinking.' Imagine that poor sap at the wheel of the old *Titanic*. He must have screamed 'Mayday' for hours before he gluggled his last glug. Glug, glug, glug, Mayday." Rollie boarded #2 singing, "Husbands and wives, little bitty children lost their lives / Oh, it was sad when that great ship went down." She was chipper again.

I wasn't. I felt abandoned by my pal. How come I'm saddled with June? She's burden enough to force "Mayday" from any stroker. I resented her more. Her calm, daydreaming figure in the bow got me sick. "Listen, June. I'm yelling 'Juneday' as my distress signal. If you don't help out in this boat you'll hear it all morning." A cross swell slapped the prow. June sat fast.

"Tie on your life vests, girls. Away all boats."

I paddled sluggishly, sloppily, not even trying to impress June or anyone. I was worn out. I'd spent the night grappling with shadows, menaced by poems. Not to mention those bully rangers. They must be crazy. Except for rain and clouds and a little wind, Aretha seemed a million miles from our course down the Broad River. June wasn't any help, either. Her paddle nipped the river like a mouse tooth in cream cheese. Nibble. Nibble. Good thing a slight current sucked us along. "You'd make a wonderful tiddlywink champion with all that power in your arms, June." No answer. Nibble. Nibble. Her sun visor, a rain visor

now, bent low. What are her eyes doing? I wondered.

Despite my shiftless stroking and June's lame
digs with her blade, we schussed down the Broad
without a hitch. "Tide's running our way, luckily.
If Aretha's nearby, she must be as bushed as I am
from last night's excitement," I said as we came
even with a small key at the mouth of Broad River.
Before us the Gulf of Mexico lifted whitecaps of
greeting. Nothing spectacular. Nothing noisy except once-in-a-while thunder. A raucous clap accompanied Miss Konecky's whistle.

"We're nicely ahead of schedule, girls. How's
for a final swim here on Highland Beach? You
could almost body surf today in these combers."

"Skip it," Rollie said for us all. "Everyone lam
out to the ranger station. The fun's gone from our
trip now."

With that we started north, single-filing along
the coast. After twenty minutes our folboats got
good and spread apart. Rollie and G.C. were nowhere in sight. Through the rain I could see #3
fairly well. Lalla held her transistor aloft like a
black pennant. Weather time, I thought, glancing
at the sky, then at the mangroves along the coast.
Nothing new. Maybe the raindrops whopped us
less. Drip, not pelt.

As sweep boat, we followed #4 as best we could,
considering my mouse in the bow. June's reading
posture just didn't make it for white-water paddling. She scuffed the Gulf with her blade. Her

timing was all off. Passing an empty campsight, she looked at me over her shoulder—maybe for instructions. Big deal. I couldn't be bothered with advice. I dug down for both of us. I kept mum as #4 drew farther and farther ahead. Then, when Bette's back made a right angle with a jut of land, disappearing mysteriously only a hundred yards away, I cut loose on the poet. "There's no other way to tell you this," I said roughly. "You're a failure—a boating washout, a camping creep. I'm sick of watching you tickle water. A headache—that's what you're giving me. Not your average two-aspirin type, either. More like a hurricane in the brain. You're dead weight! If you don't lay into these waves, I'll beach us and ditch you. The rangers can find you. Or not find you. Who cares!"

"Crash, have a heart" is all she answered. She didn't turn around.

Maybe she can't hear well. So why bother? She's hopeless. I picked up my stroke, seeking to bring #4 into view again. "Put your paddle down. You're only messing up my rhythm with those frantic plops."

Then, round a point and into the wide mouth of a creek, we caught the others where they'd waited. "You're not to be believed. Fifteen minutes behind. You're holding us back something fierce," Rollie snarled.

"Does it look like my fault, MacMaster? Number One's weighted down with your emergency equipment, and I'm paddling solo. Shall I toss out those heavy bags to lighten my load? Your first-aid . . ."

"Push out the baby. She's worth less than a snake bite kit."

"Scarcely another mile or so to the tower. Try to stay together across this open water." Miss Konecky gave June an encouraging smile.

Rollie said, "Pitch me your painter, Crash, and I'll hitch us up. Number Two'll tow Number One." She cupped her hands for the catch.

"Oh, no you don't. I can make it under my own power." I frowned back hard. "Crash power."

June helped by sitting still—her best trick—while I turned my paddle blade into a scalpel. Careful strokes. Almost dainty. Precision. On the nose, the Gulf nose, each one. Deep but delicate thrusts that kept us up and kept us on course. We soon struck our target, the ranger station at First Bay, where Lostmans River flows into the Gulf. We skidded through mud flats and kelp, went ashore shouting, "We're here early. How's that for helpless girls? Aretha's a phantom." No one called back. We footed around, looking for rangers. "Maybe those guys were just a bad dream last night," I said to the gang, a forlorn bunch of wet heads stationed humpbacked on a rickety porch.

Miss K. said, "They're probably out on other rescues. Let's fold up our boats while we wait. We'll bag them and be all ready for the trip home."

Mary Ann and Bette groaned. Lalla just squatted there, trying to fluff up her sideburns. "My hair's had a nervous breakdown," she said wistfully. G.C. allowed as how she could not get up again. June read. Tireless Rollie struck out to investigate the trees. "I'll find another manchineel. A real one. Haul some sap home to my summer English teacher. In this canteen." She emptied it in anticipation. "C'meer, Crash, and watch these strangler figs twine around their victim trees. You can almost see their roots growing with your naked eye. They're all over the place. Vicious as snakes. Another killer in the Everglades."

I was feeling low in my mind, melted by the rain, by our bombed-out trip. I said, "Rollie, come on back and just me and you will take one more ride—one for the road. A regular swashbuckler. Up there on First Bay."

"Only if we can race. You in Number One, me in Number Two. I'm getting used to that beauty. It's lighter, balancier."

"Naturally, pal. It doesn't carry all your big-time rescue junk." Then I clammed up for fear Rollie would get mad and not want to paddle again. I didn't feel like racing, but since it would be our last . . .

"These strangler fig leaves are just the right touch for your boat christening, Crash. Take them." Rollie thrust thick, oily, dark-green leaves toward my hands. Small reddish-purple flowers clung to their stems. Chaffy. Scaly. I balled up my fingers. "Take them! No? Okay, I'll paste the lot to your prow, right on top of those shriveled floating hearts. Maybe they'll seed themselves, sprout, wind around Number One and strangle her like they snuff out trees." She gave a sort of fiendish chortle and high-tailed for the boats. I followed.

"What are you up to now?" called Miss K. from the porch.

"A good-bye ride."

"Our last ride for many moons."

"Positively not!"

"A quickie."

"No, Rollie."

"Just till the rangers arrive."

"Crash, no."

"Summer school's waiting."

"Poetry's calling."

"One final lip-smacking race upstream."

"No!"

"Into First Bay."

"No!"

"Within whistle distance."

"Within your sight."

"Within your smelling range."

"No. No. No."

"Almost within touch!"

"NO."

"We'll take June for ballast."

"Now hang on, Rollie. That's going too far." I snorted.

"For ballast. For referee. To hold us back. To spy on us. To keep us in view of Nature, Inc. To save us, ha ha."

"If she goes, she's with you, Rollie," I bellowed.

"Absolutely not. June's tired. She isn't up to racing. Or spying. Let her alone."

"Come on, June. You can read."

"Be a sport, June pal. You can read *aloud*. Emily.

Edna. Elizabeth. Eleanor. June, even. That poem about love pulling her underwear on. I never heard how it ended up." Rollie started a belly laugh, then threw a hand over her mouth.

"MacMaster takes a vow of silence," I said. "For the entire race. If June comes, not a word. Except maybe praise of certain rhymes." I covered my own mouth a minute. "And cheers for love themes."

June sat still, watching us bail our racers. Miss Konecky looked at her and shrugged, as though she considered the matter settled. I tried once more to unsettle it. "Bring your books," I called. "They'll even up the weight." To Rollie I whispered. "Our logic, our promises aren't working this time, Ace. She'll never fall for . . ."

June stood up, stepped carefully off the porch, and came toward us. "Those floorboards seep rain and the tar-paper roof leaks. I might as well be in the open air with you." Her gray eyes, stamped with hope, met ours. "I'm not your ordinary dead weight," they seemed to say.

Rollie mutely helped her into the bow of #2. Then I transferred June's luggage to #1, stacking a suitcase and duffle bag on the bow seat. I lashed them to the seat back. "That's my June—winter coat, shoulder-strap purse, and the *Encyclopedia of Poetry*, a billion volumes." I patted the pile, found it secure, untied the painter, grasped the paddle once again by my blisters, and nudged off the mud. Rollie and June tailed me.

"Only within eyesight and earshot," cautioned Miss Konecky from the shore.

"Go up in the tower and umpire our race. Drop your hat for starters," Rollie called loudly, for we were moving away from the station rapidly.

"She'll get hit by lightning up there," I said, aware of clobbering thunder. I looked back toward the clustered shapes, now merging into one dark bulk under a sloping roof. No one climbed the tower. I'd start the race myself. "Take your mark. Get set. Go."

Rollie said, "I'm gone," and flashed by me, untroubled by her extra bundle.

I dug in a final time. I pulled hard. I pulled deep. Harder. Deeper. I strained forward, bent in half, shoulders nearly butting my thighs. Whitecaps slung themselves at the tight vinyl hull. Foam clung to the gunwales. Crossframes creaked in their grooves. All the interlocking aluminum rods squeaked in time to my stroking tune. Brass hinges, sliding latches, snap locks, grip handles seemed to rub against their screws, squealing, "Faster. Faster. Catch 'em." Every inch of varnished wood appeared lathered for the race, the catch.

But the lather was rain, the squeaking a whistle somewhere behind us, far in the west. And the catch? Impossible! Number Two flew ahead, Rollie's hunkered-over body like an automaton in the stern. Splish. Splash. Splish. Splash. Her two-bladed paddle hummed to First Bay. Her big paws flicked it inanoutinanout as if it were an eight-foot toothpick. Foot by foot. Yard by yard. Ahead in the rain. I followed her holler.

"Say *uncle*," she commanded the waves. "Say

uncle," she ordered the wind. "Say *uncle,*" she cried to the sheets of water now pouring from black and blue clouds. "Say *uncle,* Aretha. Say *uncle,* Crash. You've had it."

Behind, way behind, a whistle shrieking *uncle,* a girls' chorus of *uncles.* My own mind seized the word. "I give up" came straight from my brain muscles. My mouth arranged the letters. My lips parted to the "U." My teeth unclenched, my jaw stretched. My vocal chords formed the perfect *uncle.* "Unc!" I burst out. Thunder smothered my voice.

Rollie never heard the half word. She slowed, but only to toy with me. I paddled on up, next, then *wham,* she shot away, stunning Lostmans River with paddle blows. "Say *uncle,*" she said lazily, when I'd caught up again. She'd let me.

I said, "U."

"Say it all."

I said, "U—N."

"The rest. The rest."

I said, "U," then "N—C."

"Get it together—the whole word. Say it."

"U." We paddled almost abreast while I said that obscure member of the alphabet again: "U." Her painter nipped ahead of mine. "N." My garland of floating hearts, revived in the heavy rain, prowed ahead. "C." Rollie's white shirt, a stern banner, whisked by. "L," I shouted, almost in June's ear. "E." There!

"Pronounce it. Use your Dade County nasal drawl. Say it, say it."

We had reached a slight bend in the river. Intent on bending with it, I sealed my lips and opened my lead. Sand bars dotted the water. I dodged three, four, five, then passed between two kidney-shaped ones in the narrowing Lostmans. Shoals to come, I noticed, looking due east instead of at my knees. For a change.

"North of that crook—Second Bay," Rollie said to my back. "You'll never arrive. I'll devour you in my jet stream as I rocket by. This is the moment for *uncle*. Say it. Say it. You're skunked."

"Don't say it," whispered June, all even. "I've a plan."

"Say *uncle*," said Rollie to my profile.

June shook her head in a "No."

"Holler *uncle* to my ponytail," grunted Rollie, passing.

June's sopped hair, plastered like a brown helmet to her scalp, moved gently right and left. "No." Then right. Right only. I looked right at a sandy blur, poking out from a veil of vines and creepers. I looked again at June in #2, now a whir herself, crouching on heels, up, kneeling, rising, half upright, up, standing, wobbling, erect, tipping, leaning, leaning overboard, overboard, oversand—a motion picture of madness, a motionless figure on the sand bar. "Help me, Rollie, I fell."

"Like hell you fell," Rollie jeered as she slowed and backwatered. "Now Crash will grab the lead, get way ahead, win. She'll be to Third Bay by the time I fish you . . ."

"Exactly," I called, wavering, weaving between

sandy June and #2. "You're the victim of a master plot." I darted ahead. "Me and the poet did a deal." Number One pulling away. "You'll have to counter with a Rollie plan."

"I'm not wrecking my boat on this sand bar. I'm not landing." A surly blurt from Rollie. "June, I'm chucking you the painter. Grab-hold. I'll tug you into midstream. Easy boarding." Less surly. "That's it. Take it." Patient voice. "Let yourself go. I'll do the work. I'm paddling backward." Downright cheery. "Hang on. Attagirl."

I streaked around the bend, looking forward to untroubled waters. No backward glances. I'm out of sight anyway. More to my taste. Make way, all you critters. Cut and run, bobcats. Flap it, birds. Buzz off, sand flies. Here's Crash coming up the home stretch. Crashing the finish line. North into Second Bay. Out of #2's sight for good.

"Juneday! Juneday!"

Still in earshot.

"Juneday! Juneday!"

Still. In earshot.

"Juneday!" June's voice. A sudden blow to my eardrum.

"That'll teach you, baby. It's deep here, right? Maybe like eleven feet? How's drowning for a Mac-Master plot?" Her voice sounded water-choked. Lightning to my heart.

I withdrew my paddle from the bay and propped it upright against a hip. Spume trickled over the rubber drip ring, into my lap, onto my life jacket. I listened with all my might. I thought till my temples throbbed like the tides. Could Rollie be in trouble? She hadn't worn her life jacket to race. Or had she? Narrowing my eyes, I glimpsed her white tennis shirt, a hole over her heart where the alligator once crawled, grimy collar and sleeve bands ragged—a bedraggled flag of surrender. No orange puff on top. No jacket! Could she survive the river without it? And June? Where was her jacket? Back on the porch—a pillow? Inside my head I saw her mauve blouse. Mauve, yet! An old-lady color. For weddings, not heroics in the river. Only the bride's mother wears mauve. Yet now June swam in a mauve blouse. No orange vest covered it.

June can't swim in deep water. I opened my eyes. Before them, draped over #1's bow seat, June's life jacket, tied to her gear. June will drown midstream. And Rollie?

I lowered my paddle. I swept it left, left, left, left. The boat came about with startling fleetness. At once, prow downstream, I tore at the water. My blade gouged the Bay, then the Lostmans. I ripped ahead. I took ruthless, violent swings at my enemy, the river. I flogged logs, floating beer cans and Clorox bottles, schools of fish, a tiny yellow bird—whatever got in the way of my rioting paddle. Gallons of water swept by. Acres of mangroves bannered past the corners of my eyes. I searched the stormy horizon for a brown head, mauve shoulders, white hands beckoning help. Through blankets of rain I hunted my tempestuous pal. If only I'd see her kayak. "Look for your mate, Number One. Find Number Two," I shouted to my own boat. "Rollie, where are you? Mist's rising. Give a whistle."

"J u n e d a y." Dead ahead. A quavering voice.

I slowed. I peered through water into water. I coasted.

"Wheet. Wheet. Wheet." Blasty as ever. Off my port side.

"June. Rollie. Don't mess around. Another dose of murk and we'll find ourselves lost for good."

All of a sudden Rollie's torso loomed out of the fog. I nearly rammed #2's hull in happy surprise. I sheared off, saying. "Oh, wow, Rollie, am I ever glad to see you, if only your shirt." She slung her painter to me in greeting. I swung alongside, my prow to her stern. We sat face to face, grinning a lot. Finally I said, "Where's June?"

"Overboard, where she threw her own self. I towed her right here for punishment. To frighten her. A big scare. A joke. Let her stew in this steamy juice a while."

"A while?" I listened for thrashing. "A *while?*" No splashings except torrential rain. "She's been treading for minutes. She can't really swim. She's got no strokes. She's not strong like us."

"Tough."

"Rollie, come on."

"Crash, you come on."

"Rollie, help her. Hurry."

"Nope, not right now."

I began to tremble. My boat danced under me. "Rollie, you can't mean that." I met her stony gaze. "Oh, Rollie, you are heartless."

She shrugged. "You've never been noted for your sweet soul either, pal. We're the exact same . . ."

"Heartless. Heart . . ."

"So are you, even if your name is Valentine." She laughed in my face. "Mushy name." She strong-armed my boat from hers. I drifted.

Behind me, "Juneday." Murmured. I twisted in my seat. Wan hands flapped on the Lostmans. No head poked up. No wedding blouse. Just two small hands.

"Rollie, ahead of you. June's hands." I took off my life jacket and tossed it there.

"She's surface diving."

"She's not diving. She's drowning. Sling your cushion, your seat back, a crossframe—anything!"

"How about my bowie knife," she answered, beginning to paddle downstream. Or upstream. Or for the north bank. Or the south. Who could tell in the shapeless fog? Her fading snarl said, "I'll race you down to the ranger station. This time for keeps." A pause. "After you save the baby." She vanished.

I drifted. Water beat me in a vertical downpour. Raindrops like fists clubbed my head, numbed my mind, filled my mouth when I opened it to yell, "June? Where are you? June? Where arrrrrrrrr . . ." I gurgled.

Two hands again broke the surface. Starboard. Muddy bangs next, then wild and mournful eyes sought mine through a frenzy of water. June's doomed head bobbed once, down.

I jackknifed for her. I went for that head. I grabbed for a hank of hair, but only weeds filled my hands. I flailed the Lostmans, trying to touch June. I came up for air. I cried, "Help! Help me save you," and fled underwater again, breaststroking through reedy tangles. Deathly quiet replaced the storm. I'd ditched Aretha's foreshadow on the surface. I roamed the mucky bottom with flutter kicks, heart thumpings—the only sounds in that H_2O grave. It's futile, I told myself, rising for air again. Futile! I hiccuped and swallowed. She's had it.

On the surface a hand whispered to mine: June's, cold against my bulging blue veins. In an instant I jammed one hand in the hollow of her back, one between her shoulder blades, lifting her halfway out of the river. She can drown herself in rain, I thought, bracing my knees firmly under her back, freeing both hands to cup her chin and start dragging dead weight to the shore.

She didn't struggle. She seemed unconscious, dead maybe. Exhaling? Inhaling? My hands a hearse? I released my hold, braced her, and slapped her face hard. Again. Red discs appeared on her cheeks. Blood dripped from her nose. She opened her eyes to my descending palm. Slap. She panicked, clasped my neck, tried to struggle me under. She fought for her life. I fought for ours. We scuffled on the surface. I was exhausted, she filled with terminal strength. Evenly matched, we pulled each other down. With sinking hearts, two flesh persons clung together, awaiting the final spiral.

"June," I shrieked through an avalanche of water. "You're safe . . ."

We hung there, enmeshed in a clump of bubbles. Then I bit her wrist. Ferociously. I felt my molars touch bone. June relaxed her arms, released me, trailed her hands loose.

We rose. I laid hold of those mousey bangs and swam us shoalward. There's sand banks and mud keys in every direction, I remembered from the race. I gripped hope. I took heart. Dolphin kicking, swinging one arm in a wide, watery arc, I forced our path through the Lostmans.

"Your wrist tastes like beach plums," I yelled to buoy my passenger. June blinked a reply. "Your ears smell like pond apples." Her nose twitched. "Your hair feels like Spanish moss." For an answer, June's knees disappeared under water, then her shins. Down again—but suddenly she staggered up. Stood!

So did I. We wormed to higher ground and collapsed among mangroves. I grasped and clutched my stomach, aware now of wrenching cramps. At length I crawled over to June's body to have a look for vital signs. I bent close, inspecting her grayish lips. Her breath came sweet against my neck. "June, you've got cookies on your breath. After all that."

She smiled. She whispered, "Rollie gave me some Mallomars on our way up here. To keep me quiet, I suppose."

We fell asleep.

JUNE 4th

LATER

And woke to rain. Heavier than ever. Water seemed to rush at us from all sides. Blinding us. Dulling us. Drowning us ashore.

We lay on our backs—heads, elbows, calves, ankles propped up by mangrove roots. Our other parts reclined in slime. June wheezed and coughed and blew her nose. On what, I wondered, drawing myself up by a low-slung branch.

She'd read my mind. "My handkerchief—back pocket. Better than Mrs. Browning's sonnet." She blew. "To catch blood, that is."

"Don't blow, stupid. You'll only irritate the blood vessels more. Your nose is all plumped up from where I slugged you." I watched her sop rain with the lace-edged hankie, squeeze out the red, and blow again.

"Can't breathe—won't stop running."

"Let it clot, June. I didn't save your life so you could commit suicide. Tilt your head back. The gunk'll slop into your throat. Then spit. Either that or I'll have to stick a tourniquet on the tip of your nose."

She obeyed but coughed even more. And sniffled. And said, "Can't breathe."

"Turn over. Lie face down. You're shipping water through your nostrils." She obeyed. She sneezed a while but didn't choke. Muck absorbed her blood.

"Better," she panted.

"Got any more cookies? In your same pocket? I can reach them. Or elsewhere? I'm hungry. I suppose we've missed lunch."

"My suitcase—Number One—M and M's—Malted Milk Balls—Hershey Kisses—if they haven't melted."

I shielded my eyes against rain and squinted toward the Lostmans. Waterspouts or geysers or ground fog or mist or clouds or twilight or night or pea soup blocked my view. Or Aretha. "Where is she now?" I mumbled to the gloom.

"Who? Rollie? I've been asking myself . . ."

"No, Number One, filled with food. We could eat lunch while we wait for the rangers." I tried to peer through layers of Aretha, there in the very heart of the Everglades. Hope those guys come soon. Hope they can see us better than I can see . . . Or hear. We should . . . We gotta . . . We must shout. "Shout, poet. Clear your throat, lay back your ears, and shout. Else they'll miss us. We'll miss them in the storm. We'll starve."

I rocked back on my haunches and bellowed. June joined me at the waterline, scrubbing away at her face, caked with muddy blood. She peeped a few "Please helps." She sputtered. "Here we are, ranger. Over here, sirs. On the north bank. Or south. Anyway, advance toward my voice." I could hardly hear this—and I was only millimeters from her mouth.

"You're demented if you think a mouse squeal will be heard above this hurricane," I bawled between "Help, you guys."

She upped her voice—from a squeak to a squeal. "We're here, sirs." Her face turned a vivid purple from the effort. Her nose gushed again. Her rubbery legs gave way, and she settled suddenly in coily roots. She regarded me with mist-gray eyes. "I'm afraid I'm not much of a yeller." She hung her head.

"What are you much of?" I shrieked amid "Helps." My own voice began to crack. I leaned back for a drink of rain to revive my tonsils. A flash flood spun my tongue aside, water-picked my teeth, nearly swished down my windpipe, leaving me gagging and angry. "What can you do for us?" I croaked out finally. "What are you doing right this minute, for example? June, baby, we're in trouble. Have you even noticed?"

She looked slowly up at the sky. She caught eyesful of rain. She winked away pints. She said, "Yes, Crash."

"Tears aren't gonna help. We've got plenty of liquid refreshment. It's food we need. And shelter in this wilderness, before Aretha comes down on us like a demolition derby." I grabbed a leafy sapling and doubled it over. "Remember what Donna did to the Everglades? What Miss Konecky told us? About eighty-foot mangroves being toppled, torn, uprooted? What do you suppose will happen to five-four me and five-nothing you?"

No answer. I met her watchful eyes. I followed them to her hands, which traced letters in the slime. A printed FIND US SOON. A script *Crash and June*. Six words in a lopsided circle, erased by rain as my gorge rose.

"Oh, wow. You're unreal. I mean, oh June, you halfwit. It's late afternoon—evening maybe. Dinnertime. And you serve up a couplet." I clutched my head, dizzy with scorn. "A poem! We can't eat rhymes. And what about tonight? Verse won't protect our bodies from . . . Besides, you said you didn't write poems anymore."

Wind razed my mind. I went blank, blank as June. She stared at me through a rain of leaves. "I'll help, Crash," she said after a while.

I gave a lusty yelp. "Help? Help *us?* What will you do about us?"

"Anything I have to," she answered.

"Oh, if only Rollie were here."

Later.
I left off screaming and tried clapping my hands at the rangers. Seemed loud from where I sat. I kept at it. I spanked my blisters into carbuncles, wondering if sound would carry to mid-river. Probably not through that bedlam of wind and rain. I got to thinking that I should swim back out there

to holler, to hang around, to bushwhack those guys as they motored upstream. That way they couldn't pass us by. No way!

My mind was eager to dive me. My body cringed at the thought. Not now. Not again. No more sucky currents. No more chances to drown. No, I wouldn't do it. No, I won't. I say no.

"Hands up, poet. Clap with me. Or play patty-cake. We gotta attract their attention, make ourselves as noisy as their engine." My hoarse whisper must have frightened June from her reverie, for she began beating her mouse paws heartily. I saw them slap each other. I heard only squeaks. "Less namby-pamby." Tiny thuds. "Pushier. Pushier." Dinky tinkles.

"I'm sorry," she said.

I reached up and broke two long limbs from a mangrove. "Take these. Clomp 'em together." She did, weakly. "Wish we had a bell to ring. Or a gun. Or those darn cook pots in Number One. We could strike their lids like cymbals. They'd raise Cain."

"I'm trying to raise him," she said.

I thought some more. About walkie-talkies. Rollie's father had one. About police radios and sirens and floodlights—rescuers. I waggled a pulpy finger at the Lostmans. "Our folboat might be beached nearby. Our pans, flares, Tootsie Rolls—" I hadn't the mistiest idea where. "Oh, if only Rollie were here!"

You. YOU. You've got to go back into that maelstrom, I told myself. Yes, now. Yes, again.

Yes, into those jaws of water, those windfangs. Yes, you will. "Yes," I said aloud. "I say yes."

"Wait right here, June. Drum your sticks against those roots you're sitting on. Call out my name every thirty seconds. Lead me back over to this shore—this very tree."

I hurled myself forward. Once in deep water, I made my hands into tight scoops and pulled toward the opposite bank. Snags caught my sandals as I whip kicked the river. Brown suds filled my sinuses. All sorts of garbage caromed off my tensed body. Like palm fronds and pine cones. Motor-oil cans. Wine bottles. Light bulbs. A dozen T.V. dinner dishes. Half a chartreuse frisbee. A waterlogged rat and a dead duck. I watched those creatures scud downstream. Or upstream. I wished for a tail, for webbed feet, for fur, for feathers, for help from nature instead of the shaft. I wish to hear a motorboat, see a green uniform. Instead, I found the other shore.

But what if I did? It was exactly like the shore I'd left 100 yards behind, only more so. Tanglier branches, snakier roots, gummier mud—why had I sprinted like a maniac? No folboat. No rangers. No June. "June," I hollered. "Can you hear me?"

Nothing. Nothing unless you count a throaty howl of wind an answer. Nothing unless you consider the hail of twigs on my head a greeting. No "Crash" calls. No thwacked sticks. Only a brutal clout to my ear from a hunk of blowing debris. Some hello! "Hello," I shouted back. "Why don't

you blow in someone else's ear for a change?" The
rangers, perhaps, as they stand on the deck of their
wonderful cruiser jetting my way, only minutes
ahead of the gale to come. Oh, what's the use?

And a gale was coming, I'd grown sure of it.
"Gale-force winds," the announcer always said when
old Donna or Alma or Betsy or Hazel or Zorro spun
up from the Caribbean and blustered toward
Florida. Then he'd say stuff like "Barometer falling
to twenty-six point eighteen" or a number like
that, and "People in exposed places should move
to higher ground." Higher ground—ha! The peak
elevation in the entire Everglades measured around
four feet above sea level—five feet tops. I'd have to
climb a bald cypress—and get picked off by lightning.

And about the forecaster's "small-craft warnings." Could #1 qualify as small craft? Unlikely! A
dwarf craft, maybe. A peewee compared to the
sloops and yawls and schooners that return to har-
bor when the radio says "small craft." I stroked a
toy boat by comparison—and where was it, by the
way? I'd never find it in time to beat Aretha's flags
to the poles. "Remember, the hurricane warning
flag is bright red with a square black center . . ."
I'll bet it's flying now from Key Largo to Fakahat-
chee Bay. "The eye of the hurricane will pass
twenty-five miles east—or west—or directly . . ."
What eye? What is an eye? Where? When? What
color could it be? I eagled the sky, three inches
above me. Gray. It'll have gray eyes, like June.

"June," I called. "I'm coming back. Wait up. Stay cool. I'm on my way." I set out again.

Uffff. Right at me as I freestyled the Lostmans, more rubble, this time the big junk. Like a deck hatch. Like a rudder. Like a spinning deck rail. Like a boomeranging folboat—at me, away, at me, away. Caught in a whirlpool. Both of us.

I hurtled my chest out of the scum and onto the thwarts of #1. I hung on, legs dragging. Ten seconds went by. Twenty. Sixty. Mentally I ticked them off while I rode my toy like a merry-go-round. Around. Around. Where's the brass ring? Around. Around. My nickel's used up, I kept thinking. Around. Around. "*Stop* and I'll give you a nickel," I finally cried to my bobbing vinyl horse.

For an answer I heard "Crash." Feeble, but my name, all right. "Crash." Over the Niagara of water. Over the gale-force winds. "Crash." Her poor throat must be raw by now. And near. I could even make out a faint clacking that accompanied the "Crash." Nearing. Sticks clicking. June calling. Nearer. From my joy ride I watched June whirl out of the fog.

"June, grab the painter. Grab the bow. The stern. Whatever you can reach! Before I go by you."

June motioned to the painter as it circled by her saddle oxfords. She made a move toward the bow. Too slow. She gestured meekly at the bow-seat bundle. Not fast enough. She leaned and reached for my right arm, which was stretched amidship in a death grip. Zilch. I tried to backwater my legs, to lessen #1's roundabout progress. I spun in that alien zone crying, "June, latch on, don't let me downriver." She leaned farther, made a pass at my left hand where it clung to a crossframe. I felt her fingers slide by. She leaned farther, then farther, jabbing her sticks at my fists. I opened up. I snatched. I closed my left hand over these offerings, pulled, pulled my pony for shore. "Good thinking," I cried, landing us both on a sand bar. "Poet, your adrenalin must be pumping like crazy. You did it."

"I had to."

"You hung tough. Almost as good as Rollie."

Still later.

"At least we'll die on full stomachs," I announced to Aretha after a supper of Mary Janes, marmalade, Cheeze Whiz, Boston brown bread, and sponge cake. A very spongy affair altogether. We'd raided every food source aboard #1—June's Samsonite, Rollie's grub box, my watertight dry packs, even a small pouch of Lalla's, left behind when she transferred to #3. "She won't need these doughnuts. She's home and safe and hunking down barbecue by now. Over to the country club with . . . Wonder if Aretha is doing a number there, too."

June said nothing.

"Eat more, Regan. Get up your blood sugar. Extra energy. Then you'll be able to help me set off Rollie's flares. You hold 'em, I'll light 'em. We'll have fireworks for dessert."

June said, "Okay," and unwrapped another Tootsie Roll.

"I'd sooner be a corpse from drowning or snakebite than from starvation," I added, looting Lalla's pouch for one last cruller.

She chewed.

"That blouse of yours is little more than confetti. The Lostmans tossed you . . ."

She mused.

"Guess your glasses and sun visor went to Davey Jones's locker when you jumped . . ."

She gazed at the river.

"What you thinking about, Regan? Some dinner companion you are! Okay, your throat's sore from shouting; but how about a word, a complete sentence—that sort of thing. A poem."

"I don't . . ."

"I know. You don't write anymore. Say why while I find the flares." I frisked Rollie's emergency bag until I touched a foil package. I pulled it out and felt for the matches. Rollie always stored them in an unbreakable thermos bottle—to keep them dry. Ah, there. "You're not confessing, June. No Fourth of July until you say why. What's your secret?" I couldn't really care less what or why, but I felt lonely there in the bloodthirsty Everglades with no one to shout back at me.

"Crash, I've something to tell you. Do you mind?"

I grunted and peeled foil. "Hurry up, before these get wet."

"Concerning the river. It's rising up quickly. I've been watching the waterline on those roots." She pointed at the nearest mangrove, right beside the one I'd chosen as green armor while we waited for our rescuers. We were curled up in its low branches, #1 tied below us.

"So it's rising up. We'll climb higher. Hold this end while I strike a match. You're about to see stars right through the gloom."

"I trust the rangers will, too." She seemed ruffled by her observation, not quite herself. She fidgeted.

Soon great balls of fire rained in the rain as I lit one signal flare after another. "Puts me in mind of Roman candles," I jabbered to myself. Gusts caught the sparks, sending rosy showers east or west, to the station or to Big Lostman's Bay. "Whoopee! Not bad for that sludgy sky. Plus, their wrappers are damp."

June watched the river. "Maybe those men passed us while we lay asleep," she called over a fizzling fuse.

"This here's a dud. Powder's wet. Only one more left." Under Rollie's oilskin slicker I struck a final match. The fuse caught, held, sent its message aloft in a hail of embers.

"How long might we have slept?"

"Can't say without Rollie's watch. I never wear one. I always ask her." I screwed the cap back on the thermos. "That's the end of our . . ."

" 'This is my letter to the World / That never wrote to Me— . . .' "

JUNE 4th

EVEN LATER

Chuting along. We move so easily, steady wind behind us, currents and tides and whirlpools and eddies sucking us with them. We seem to travel in several directions at once. Counterclockwise with buzz-saw speed. Straight forward in bubbly haste. Now and then the water runs smooth, us slick as if on ball bearings. Whush. Whush. Whush. Whush. I give up trying to keep tabs on our course. I give in to my urges of the moment: watch fog break up in patches; watch flotsam wash against the hull; watch rain squirt our prow; watch June bale and watch.

"Oil stains on the right," she calls.

"Starboard."

"Snake swimming left."

"Port. Don't trail your hands as you dump the can. You'll get bit."

"Dead raccoon in front. Totally bloated."

"Dead ahead."

"We're surrounded by boat pieces. And drowned birds. Oh, Crash, I hate to see these mangled limpkins. They're scarce enough as it is."

"Snuffed out by Aretha, I suppose. What's a limpkin?"

I consider our tailwinds. Growing rambunctious now. Puffing us downstream, my paddle as rudder. Freshening our spirits as we sled whitecaps. Blowing us home. Haze lifts. Hope lifts.

"First Bay must be under that shadow ahead," I sing out.

"Um."

"Lostmans seems skinnier than when we stroked up. But then I was racing, not noticing all that much."

"Yes, it's narrower. Right here, at least. I can see both banks."

"Fog's passing."

"Night's falling instead. Grackle black, judging from the clouds. No moon at all."

"Or stars—even if I could read 'em. So much for celestial navigation."

I consider our route. Meandering south? Drifting westward? Must get our bearings before dark happens. No landmarks. All these blasted mangroves the same color—height—bushiness.

"Wish we had Miss Konecky's maps."

"Um."

"I don't recognize these zigs and zags. Lostmans seemed straighter."

"Yes, it was. Arrowy, compared to this."

"Widening. There! Bay coming on."

"Not vast enough for First Bay."

"Can't see to the end. Might be. June, scrounge

up your flashlight. Mine, too. And Rollie's in her gear. Throw some volts ahead."

"Would this compass be of use? Right here with my flashlight."

"Where? Rollie always wears hers."

"Mine."

"I forgot about yours. Pass it back."

I consider the compass. Faded face. Little. Is the needle spinning? Or our boat? Both! Number One kinks around a key, skates straight, then curves a great curve, avoiding dunes of sawgrass. I try to take a fix on our position. The needle lands north, the dial shows us coursing east, southeast, east, northeast, east, south, southeast. North behind us. North off the portside. North in darkness.

"Your compass is busted. We can't be moving east."

"Um."

"We gotta be headed southwest, downriver with the Gulf tide . . ."

"Tides turn."

"Toward the ranger station with the current . . ."

"This wind seems stronger than any current we've met in the past four days. It keeps shifting."

"It's mauling my back."

"Crash, duck. Foliage overhead. Break our necks at the rate we're going."

"I can't see a thing."

I consider our vision. Me doubled down, trying

to paddle. June without glasses. Both in bruisey blueblackness, now mixed with concussions of rain. We breach a wall of branches. The boat sluffs off mud, enters a tunnel of trees, careens along a viny right bank. Briars rake our arms until open water again.

"Off the starboard bow. We'll hit it!"

"Um."

"Sit tight for the crunch, June."

"It's a channel marker."

"How can you see?"

"Far-sighted. Glasses for reading."

"Read that marker. Shine your beams."

"Number forty-one."

"Where could we be?"

"Big Lostmans Bay. Or Third Bay."

"You gotta be kidding."

"I remember the numbers."

"You're amazing, June."

"I recall the forties markers all through these two inland bays. The same numbers as in Cormorant Pass. I studied the map at . . ."

"Wait'll Rollie hears that."

I consider our problems. Blown east. Inland four, maybe six miles. No way to dodge the wind. No chance of retracing my strokes downstream. Not now. Will the rangers find us here? Can they sleuth us out in the dark? Are they even looking in this storm? Rivulets of black water roll off June's shredded blouse. She aims the flashlight east.

"At this rate we'll be whipped clear across Florida tonight," I holler.

"Um."

"Come out the other side—at Key Biscayne."

"Not likely. We'll probably run aground at a hummock."

"I can climb trees there. Boost you up. Rope us to the top."

"Rocks off portside. Way underwater . . ."

"You gotta be kidding."

"Jagged ones," she adds.

"First rocks of this trip."

"Limestone entrance to Rocky Creek—on the map."

"Regan, you're unreal. How do you remember? Reach in my rucksack for my new windbreaker. Put it on over that blouse."

I consider our plusses. Plenty of grub. A tent if we can find high-enough ground to pitch on. Blankets if the wind turns cold. Ropes, first-aid kits, clothes in my dry packs, all Rollie's life-saving treasures under the bow. Everything but an ice-cream freezer. We can live off the land—the water—if worst comes to worst. Loads of belly-up fish floating around us.

"Eat your heart out, Aretha. We're not licked yet."

"What?"

"We're simply taking a roundabout way home, Regan. Scenic cruise."

"Don't crash into these snags starboard."

"Our minds went in one direction, our boat in the other."

"Crash, these snags . . ."

Snaggling along. We move haltingly, driving wind behind us, but treefangs and deadheads and wreckage and rocks holding us, tearing at our hull. We seem to be traveling into oblivion. Submerging on an unswerving course. Earthward in an unsteerable boat. Up and down we rock in the merciless water, rain pummeling our heads as if to slam our brains out through our teeth. Crash. Crash. Crash. Crash. I feel the boat fill up with Rocky Creek. I feel #1 run aground.

"Regan, we're lost in a hurricane," I howl to June as we crawl for higher turf. "What can we do now?"

"Anything we have to."

We give back yell for yell to the wind.

JUNE 4th or 5th

Last night? Or is it today already? Our next day?
Our same night in Aretha?

We yanked #1 up on a rocky tongue that licked
the rising water. In darkness broken only by rays
from our flashlight we searched through gear and
covered our rain-chewed clothes with outfits soaked
as they emerged from packs. We pulled on sweat-
ers, jackets, parkas as if cloth alone might protect
us from the murderous elements. Then I grabbed
ropes and ground cloths, intent on tying us in mangroves, winding us with plastic and rubber and
canvas shrouds. I fastened the boat to an armful of
branches. I knew it could never float again. Rips in
the bottom, slits along the sides, crossframes bat-
tered nearly to sawdust, it lay like a dying girl,
slashed by sharks, butted by whales. It served as a
wilderness cupboard now, holding our food and
equipment—our lifeline.

With careful hands over hands we climbed the
closest tree, a little one. Wind rattled this refuge,
causing us to pause short of the top: June and Crash
at half mast, two trippers suddenly cast pellmell

to the sawgrass below as limbs broke in a terrible gust. We lay under crackling branches.

Time stammers, stands still. Who knows what time it is? After awhile I thought, Come on, Regan. We can't hide here in the mud. We'll drown. I got up and walked, my back toward the creek. East? West? June followed without a word. Ground held us like tar. With maddening slowness we wrenched each footstep from it. Fine teeth on the tall thin grass snicked our pants, gradually tore cotton, exposing leg skin. Soon enough we bled into our shoes from a mess of fresh scratches. Water entered our muscles as we plodded across the 'Glades. We tired more. Heads down against the gale, we scarcely noticed an abandoned heap of alligator eggs in a stick and leaf nest. The mother must be around here someplace, I thought, narrowly missing a stomp on her offspring—about eighty ping-pong balls leaking yolks in the storm. Would she get me back like the snake mate? What if she does? Her teeth? Aretha's? Does it matter?

We faltered and stalled and flailed and halted in the porous muck. We gazed ahead in thick dark, noting nothing. We shivered in our yeasty shoes. In a reflex we turned collars up against Aretha.

A noise riveted our attention—a dozen booming roars. From—from an alligator, sure enough. We lifted feet and started again, turning right, away from the dragon. His bellow tracked us through tufts of grass. We mushed, scared.

Trees thinned to none. Only sawgrass grew in

our way. It, sharp as broken glass, high as head-lights. It bit our thighs now. We kept mushing.

The spell of the storm fell on us. Rain dunked our spirits. Wind tore at our hearts. In our despair we nearly shuffled past a raised piece of land over-grown with trees—a hummock in this cruel marsh. With eyes adjusted at last to the dark we saw palms toppled in heaps, but some yet standing. We saw strangler figs torn from their victims but twisting instead around the pitched roof of a cabin—a shack really, wallowing beneath a tall tree with reddish brown bark. We heard a door slap shut, then open with a pock. SLAP. POCK. A welcome noise. We plucked up courage, determined to make better weather of it.

We traipsed from mudgrass to humus to shack door. POCK. SLAP. POCK. We slipped in. I spread the one tarp that wind hadn't stolen from my fists. June flopped first. Her profile on the ground had one shut eye, one white ear, half an open mouth, half a bleeding nose. She needs her head tipped, I thought, feeling around for a pillow. I touched puddles, glass, boards, metal, feathers. I touched a cold—long—scaly—snake. Must be. Dead, or I'd be. I threw a weak beam of flashlight on the body. Yes, quite dead. What species alive? What matter?

SLAP. POCK. Out again for leaves, pine needles, moss, flowers—anything pillowy. Fronds too stiff. Pine cones too hard. I gathered ferns from Aretha, bunched them in my sweater, darted back with a pock, lifted June's head, wiped her nose. "Not exactly a snuggery," I cried over the hurricane, "but for sure we won't be attacked by an abominable snowman." In half sleep she laughed as if her heart might break.

JUNE 5th

Now we are talking to each other. At moments almost mouth to ear—to hear—we lie in scribbles of light let in by the rotting walls.

"Good morning, Crash. Or good noon."

"Good day. That should cover it."

"I feel better—not as weary."

"You slept like a bear."

"Didn't you? Sleep? Any?"

"I watched you bleed until I ran out of flashlight. Then I listened to animals scuttle around this piggery. Take a look."

She did. A glance that brought on a gasp that turned to a long gigglegroan. "Oh Cra-sh. Crash."

The filthy, wrecky cabin sheltered critters swept in by Aretha. Us and turtles made one heap. Mangrove squirrels and grass frogs another. Toads hopped everywhere. Water rats prowled corners. Skinks lay bunched near our bed. Two bats hung upside down from the rafters. A storm-rumpled vulture shook his tail and pointed his hooked bill and talons at our flesh. "We're not dead yet, bustard," I told him. "So stop drooling. And don't get your hopes up. If we kick the bucket, so do you."

"He's harmless while we're alive. He's more afraid of us than . . ."

"How 'bout that skunk on the bench? He could stink us right out of here, through the hummock, back to the boat." I reached to hold my nose. That abrupt motion caused a 'possum to bolt from a spindly chair and into the shadow of a pot-bellied stove. Several shrews followed him. Minks moved over, their yellow eyes sparkling. "We're aboard Noah's ark. I wonder if it leaked, too." I dropped my hand from nose to tarpaulin. An inch of water had collected under us and the snappers since June opened her eyes. "Chilly in this kiddie swimming pool."

"But lighter than I expected. There's sun behind the clouds. The center of Aretha must not be coming our way."

"Or if it is, not till later." The sudden coolness means something, I thought, but no use alarming June. I gave her my best reassuring smile. She smiled back. "What's for breakfast?" I asked. "Poems don't count."

She smiled wider. She said, "Just as I came awake I thought of a line of poetry—several lines."

"Yours? Your own ones for a change?"

"Yes . . . no . . . partly."

"Let me guess. A Dickinson-Regan combination. Heavy on the Emily. Am I right?"

"No . . . yes . . ." She broke off and brushed her hand across my scalp. "Mice on you. Climbing."

My hair roots tingled. "I'll kill 'em, kill 'em." I swatted my head. I ran assassin's fingers over my braids. "They've got nerve."

"Crash, if we stay still—right here—perhaps all these creatures will keep their distance."

I wanted to find a chair rung and bust a few guys in the snout. I wondered what could be under the low table by the door. Or by the large crock on a shelf. Specters? Better not to ask; better not sit up to see. Don't frighten June, I resolved. "Okay, let's play 'possum."

"That seems best." I felt her even stiller beside me. I saw her pretend that a lizard wasn't crossing her neck. I watched her follow a flying squirrel doing his aerial act overhead, any moment to plummet into our eyes with his scratchy feet. I flinched. Not June. I noticed how she didn't stir when a black nose sniffed her jacket cuff—my jacket. I gave that muskrat a cuff of my own when he padded across my waist. "Best not to move," said June, watching fur fly.

"Teach me to be still then. You're a master of no motion."

"Why would you want to learn?"

"I've always been a mover—a shover—a crasher . . ."

"Better than being a weak, helpless mouse like me." She laughed without budging a muscle and added, "A Mouse can look at a Crasher."

I didn't wipe the next crawler away—a gecko. I tried to think of something else while it roved me lengthwise. But when a toad jumped me, I jumped him. "Uffff."

"Best not to move."

"Fine. Teach me what to think about while I stay still."

June moved, enough to blow her nose, and said, "Think about the star toes on that gecko. Think about the funny narrow mouth on that toad you pulverized. Think about the playful otter whizzing by us now. Think about the delicious mint green of these resurrection ferns you wadded under my head."

"How do you know what they are?" I asked, pulling a wilting stem from the sweater pillow-case.

"I've read of them."

"Poems?"

"Yes, and in other sources as well. They roll up in dry weather. Die a little. They come to life in the rain."

Then she showed me a pattern on a turtle shell and made me feel the ridges on its back. She pulled feathers from a dead purple gallinule and described their iridescent colors like—like a poet. When a bat fell near our bed she named it "flittermouse" and called my attention to its "handwing—four fingers and thumb covered with a web like a nylon stocking."

"I've never heard you talk so much, Regan. You ought to be a writer—a poet, maybe."

"I used to be. I loved writing . . . before . . ."

"What happened? Did you grow lazy? Writing's hard work. It gets your fingers sweaty on the pen." I looked at my right hand in the cool gloom of our hovel. No ink stains anymore. Better the blisters and chigger bites and muscles and rain and mud there. Even the blood under my nails beats a ballpoint leak. "I hate putting words down."

"Still, you do well when you try. When you care."

"How would you know?"

"English class. Themes out loud. Yours about Nature, Inc." She said "ink," not "incorporated."

"Earned me a D-plus. That woman hated everything I wrote. Hated me and Rollie. She's a cretin." Creatures around me seemed to agree. Chirrings from a stack of decaying orange crates sounded like long yeses. Crickets on my team, I thought. A tender mouse squeak—in my mussy hair again—approved my judgment. So did June.

"She's not very bright. She *liked* my poems."

"So?"

"So she shouldn't have! You and Rollie were right to laugh." Chirrings for her, too. And another sound near the table—a dry, raspy, hissing, ticking. "Yesyesyesyes," said her fans. The door gave an assenting POCK.

"I think a marsh rabbit blew in." I changed my position, sat for a better view of our companions. "I think me and Rollie should of kept our mouths shut that day. I'm sorry."

"You two did me a favor. You made me examine

my own poems." I heard more ticking. "Yes. Yes. Yes." No, not ticking. Buzzing. Rattling. Loud buzzing. Rattling under the table.

Our shelter turned suddenly to a funeral parlor. Squirrels left off chittering. Birds shut their beaks. Nobody crept or skittered or leaped or flew. No waves in the pool. Not a fourfoot stepped from his haven. Mammal ears seemed full of Aretha— and the rattle. Snake eyes held us all suspended. I saw them, finally: two laser beams, melting me from ten feet away.

"Cool it, June. Do your thing. Gentle moves. Silent. Ease up beside me. Face the door. Pierce that rattler with your own gray eyes He'll say 'uncle.' "

She sat up. She stared. "He's big." She trembled.

"A pile of coils around that table leg. Stretched out he must be about . . ."

"Six feet, possibly seven. So much longer than the one my mother ran over!"

I got less anxious. "Can't be the mate, then. Unless different species intermarry." I only half believed G.C.'s tale. "This must be the eastern diamondback. Rollie should be here to collect its rattles." That's not the only reason, either. She'd know what to do. The guy's guarding the door. What if we want to check out of here? Like back to #1 for some grub?

We looked him over from our distant bed. Black diamonds bordered with yellow ran coilwise on a greenish background. "Rather beautiful, the colors, his design," said June.

"If a killer can be pretty. See those two deep holes just in front of his eyes? Maybe *he's* been bitten!"

"Heat sensors. I read about them, too. Rattlers find their prey by detecting body heat. Rabbits are warm, and mice and voles . . ."

"And us." I watched the icy eyes stare back at June. "Don't you ever blink—either of you?"

June didn't answer. The diamondback did. He rattled and hissed, feigned a strike at a widening pool asplash with amphibians. He seemed to say, "Do not touch me," with the slender tongue that now slipped in and out of his mouth. His blunt head began weaving from side to side. His tail worked rapidly. His hackles were rising; what could be riling him? I wondered.

Outside our snake lair the wind took off on another spree. Tree limbs pelted our shelter, bunging sizable gaps in the ancient roof. Twigs, leaves, bark that fell on us appeared to have been run through a hamburger grinder. Whiffs of murky, colder air stormed our nostrils by surprise. "Something worse is happening out there." June's eyes swept away from the table leg. "And in here." She pinned them on a disorderly shelf above the stove. Mixed among tin cans and cracked bowls, pop bottles and rusty skillets, a pickle reared from a crock.

"How can a pickle lift itself?" I narrowed my eyes and looked again. "Do pickles have forked tongues?"

"A diamondback gherkin," said June. Their eyes met, held. June's wavered, then held again.

"A mate. No wonder the other guy began to sway around. He must know she's there. Maybe he's protecting her."

"Or the other way around. Right now he looks ready to slither to her side." June trembled again. The floor snake arched one-third of his body, rattled, backed to the stove, gazed up at the crock. He unhinged his jaw and hissed like an enraged gander. His friend—or mate—hung herself vinelike from the shelf answering: "Hissssssss. Hissssssss."

Overhead, underfoot. Curving forms, whirls of coils, flatheads nodding, tails wagging so fast they became blurs—the two rattlers ignored debris dropping around them.

We couldn't. Timbers flew. Roofing split June's pillow. A rafter broke from our disappearing ceiling and hit the orange crates, sending them in all directions like pick-up-sticks. The door blew inward from its frame, smeared an otter near the stove, came to rest on a cornered rat. Small dead fish and birds landed on our bed. Our own coffin? Ribbons of Spanish moss soared above us. Our funeral wreaths? The far wall shook on its foundation, tossing a tattered calendar in my lap: 1960. Hurricane Donna.

We cowered in Aretha, eyes strafing the floor, the shelf.

"Hissssssssss." Floor.

"Hissssssssss." Shelf.

HSSSSSSSSSSSSSSSSSSSSSSS. Wind like a banshee.

"That shelf's about to fall on us," June screamed in my ear.

"So's this cabin."

"Rrrrrrrrrrrrrattle." Shelf.

"Rrrrrrrrrrrrrrattle." Floor.

RRRRRRRRRRRRRRRRRRRattle. Our Everglades shack. Disintegrating. Drowning.

"June, we gotta make a run for it—past those two. Get outside before this tomb flattens us." I thrust myself up from the tarpaulin but was knocked down at once by wind through the door opening. I lay breathing water.

"We'll make a crawl for it, Crash."

She pounded my back—blows from a pussywillow. Even so, I retched up puddles, shook off a clinging newt, and came to my knees. June knelt beside me. Four hypnotic eyes kept us there. Dirty, wavy water rose around our thighs. We quailed in it. "Regan, we'll never sneak by that pair."

"We might."

"Name your poison, poet. Theirs? Or four walls crushing your spine?"

"Theirs. I'll go first."

"Aren't you afraid?"

"My heart's in my mouth."

"Mine, too. I'll go first."

"No. Unwise. I'm smaller."

"That's no advantage! Not ever."

"Most of me will be under water at the rate it's pouring in now. I can squirm outside and create a diversion."

"A diversion? You? Over this noise? Isn't a hurricane diversion enough? I mean, those killers don't even blink when a tree sails by their fangs."

"They haven't any eyelids," hollered June. "Can't blink." She started sucking lungs of extra breath, preparing to go under. She gagged on the rainy air.

"I don't want you to chance it. You'll get bit." I took June's hand and drew her closer, noticing my own teeth marks on her wrist, there from yesterday in the Lostmans. I'd chewed a broad oval welt, now yellowish around the edges, red in the middle. Wicked-looking! Could a rattler's two hypodermic needles bite worse? "Of course! His saliva's poison. Mine washed off," I blurted, pulling June closer against me just as a roof beam smacked water where she'd knelt.

She hugged me a second, then slipped my grasp, pushed herself below the froth and forward toward the doorway. Most of her stayed under water. Except her hips. I followed them while they passed a floating stool, passed a foundering mattress, passed a spinning kettle, bashed into a deadhead—but went on. A few more inches. Only a few. She'd be to the stove. She'd pass the stove. She'd pass the shelf. She'd outwit the snakes—

A rabbit vaulted water, landed on June's surfaced hips, sat on his raft, and flopped his ears. June felt him there, felt something settle itself for a ride. She wiggled her hips. The bunny wiggled his ears.

"Hissssssssss." Shelf.

"Hisssssssss." Stove, where the long one had stationed himself above the fathomless floor.

Hssssssssssss. Silt zinging the air. I'd pitched fistfuls at the rabbit, now even with the stove. I missed.

The rattlesnake couldn't. Right under his heat sensors—June and her passenger. He gave them both a lethal look, forked out his tongue, lanced the distance, and sank his fangs in. In what? In who?

I barely saw that strike and recoil. All too swift for my rain-filled eyes. I saw a left-right-left smudge and a rattler regathered on his stove. He sat quietly. He seemed satisfied with his split-second deed. He never gave a sign of what he planned to do next. June's unwiggling hips moved out of range, out of doors. Her easy rider rolled off.

Back through the door came Aretha, rushing and raging, possibly nearing her apex, stalking me in my den. "June, did you make it? June, what . . ." The wind stood up and screamed at me. And blew in a tails-down rabbit, riding an eddy now. "June, how fast does venom work? Is . . ." Cataracts swamped my tongue.

S-P-L-A-T. Another S-P-L-A-T. The deadly couple hit the water. Four teeth swam nearby.

"June, your diversion. Here's the moment!" A stunning shock of wind my answer. The snakes slithered up on a floating table.

She's out there bitten to death, paws up in the hummock. She's been poisoned and drowned at the same instant. "Oh, you villain," I wailed to the roaring water. "I hate you with all my heart. And you two butchers. I'm sick of your scaly diamonds, your curves. I'll ram your forked tongues out through your tails."

Nothing but teeth in their arsenal. Me—I've got hands and feet and fangs of my own, and boards and shingles and naily two-by-fours, I thought, watching the far wall fly apart. Ah, there's another exit.

Inside my veins adrenalin set out to hearten me. I felt blood charge my brain, rouse my will, strengthen my legs. I waded for the open end. I elbowed aside all obstacles. I laid hold of a blunt instrument—a hunk of the cabin—and bore down on my victims. They reared on their surfboard, the table half awash in our churning pond. Riding wavelets, those snakes hung five—rattles. They bounced around in a V-shaped flow, right at me.

I upped my bludgeon. Revenge and Aretha filled the air. I didn't hesitate. I crashed wood on the closest head. Pow. A hit. A flatso. Up again—mate striking—at me—

POW

CRASH

A wind-loosened rafter lambasted the surfboard. Cascading water uncoupled the roof, which fell in a plank-and-tin hail. I dove for the floor, now a lake bottom in the splintering cabin. I burrowed in sludge and stayed under in a soup of squashed animals while Aretha boomed and hissed above. I waited for the three remaining walls to crunch me. I waited for a mate bite. I waited to run out of breath. I waited with lungs fit to burst.

In a minute I thrust myself up through the carnage. I blinked away fizz. There was inky water coming from every direction. Up through soil, roots, wreckage. Sideways through bushes. Straight down through vines raveling and snapping in the tempest. One tree stood defiantly. No cabin walls stood anywhere. Gone. Sent skyward by the wrathful wind. A hooting blast tore at my braids. The only other sound an "Adams." Then unexpected silence. Then?

"Adams."

I swam through random shafts of sunlight piercing olive-green clouds.

"Adams."

I aimed for the tree, zeroed in on the trunk.

"Adams."

Grabbed a limb and leapfrogged others.

"There you are, Adams." Wrapped in vines, in the crotch of that mighty gumbo limbo, June. "Thrown here, against my will." June, unbitten. "Did he strike at me?" her only question.

"Did he ever! Must have hit the bunny."

"I watched our cabin blow to flinders."

"Yeah, poet. Some diversion you created there!" I whispered. "You do good work."

June heard in the sudden calm.

JUNE 5th

MIDDAY

"So this is the eye of a hurricane," June whispered.

"And it isn't gray, it's blue." I could see patches of open sky high over the leafless, fractured branches of our tree tower. Sun showered us now instead of rain. "And hot here."

"Sweltering. Maybe we'll dry up before the second half of the storm."

"When'll it start up again?" The smell of fresh-sloughed soil relaxed me. I gazed out over the sawgrassy lake. Water lay like wet cement. Not a ripple. A wave of hope, of joy came upon me. "Aretha's finished. She huffed and puffed and blew herself . . ."

"No, Crash, we're merely in the center of this storm. I've read about the lull . . ."

"How long does it last? Do poets say?"

"Depends on the size of the hurricane. The bigger they are, the larger the eye."

"Then we should have a peaceful decade. Aretha's been happening forever, seems like."

"Never more than an hour-long eye. Usually much less. A short recess."

"Your nose is bleeding again."

It was, too. And my ears popped, but not for long. Soon I noticed the utter silence of those Everglades. Nothing stirred. Did anything live, except us? In the hush I could hear my own hair growing. I could hear sap in our gumbo limbo. I could hear two heartbeats—one slow and even, one quick and skippy. Listening absorbed me.

For many minutes. Then watching. Butterflies appeared as if by magic. Soundlessly they winged over the blitz site that once was our cabin. They darted among vines, hovered over brush, soared to occasional stops on our limbs. June grinned with delight. Her nose stopped dripping on my braids.

"Tiger swallowtails. Mangrove skippers. Ruddy daggerwings."

"You're kidding."

"Monarchs. Queens. Buckeyes."

"How do you know? Don't tell me! You read about them in . . ."

"Southern skipperlings. Tawny emperors. Yes, I read names. I don't know what these are. Great purple hairstreaks, perhaps. Or American painted ladies. I'm only naming, not identifying."

"Neat names."

"Yes, almost poems in themselves." Butterflies landed in her shredded clothes, flowed through her sleeves, gushed out from under her feet, now bare on the barkless wood.

"Where's your shoes, poet? I hope nothing tragic happened to the only pair of saddle oxfords left in Florida."

"Mud pulled them off. Yours, too." I glanced straight down. She was right. My sandals had disappeared. My toes were slimy airstrips for specks of saffron, rose, silver, pearl, and blue. "Eastern pygmy blues, monks, cloudless sulphurs, whirlabouts. Crash, you look nice in butterfly blue—it's your color."

"You sound like Lalla with her foot make-up, ankle rings, glossy toenails. Like that." Butterflies spangled the air around my head. I tried to wave them away.

"Yellow and blue . . . butterfly headband . . . a golden blooming . . . hair roots, shoots . . ."

"My wretched hair's got the mange. It itches from sleeping in that ark." Reaching up to scratch, I knocked away an extra-heavy hair ribbon, a bird this time. It taxied to a stop on June's wrist.

"Warbler. Yellow throat. See this tiny black mask he wears? Looks like a bandit." She smoothed its feathers.

"About to stick up your bite." Her wrist welt—my bite—seemed super angry in the sun, leaning now through fluffy clouds. The warbler gave a "wichity wichity" and flittered off to join hundreds of other birds that suddenly flew in Aretha's eye.

"I suppose they're trapped in this lull. They don't dare try to escape through the wind walls."

"Come to that, neither do we. We're just as stuck."

But somehow, right then, I didn't mind. I kept my eye on the flyers, my mind off the storm. So what if any time now the winds rise again! So what if we perish with the gumbo limbo! "Husbands and wives, little June and Crash will lose their lives / Oh, it'll be sad when this great tree goes down," I sang out. Birds coasted in time to my tune. A velvety tail grazed my cheek. Deep-blue wings glided off June's brow; a cardinal stubbed his crest on her nose. "Red on red. Your blood color." I felt happy.

"Swallows. Tanagers. Wrens."

"You know them?"

"Ruby-throated hummingbirds, red-winged blackbirds, blue jays, blue grosbeaks."

"Beautiful skyriders. Mix them together and you've got purple."

"Martins. Purple martins and crows. And Crash, the meadowlarks, vireos, titmice! Oh, there's a chuck-will's widow." She nodded to a big-mouthed bird hurrying through the calm. "Yes, I know these. I'm not just naming names."

She named more, identified them, revealed them to me. She let go one hand from her hold and pointed to field marks: black caps on terns, white wing patches on mockingbirds, wide masks on chats.

"Neat name for a bird. 'Chat.' "

Her descriptions started to flow together, to rhyme a lot: soarabout redbirds / daggertheblue, owl / scowl, hawk / flock, swallow / hollow / follow, Crash / bash / dash / rash / flash. "What rhymes with Valentine?" she asked out of a clear sky—ours, overhead, all around, tinseled with birds.

"No other word. Dumb name anyway."

"It isn't either. I love the image—hearts, cupids, stinging red candies. And all. I love your real name."

"Birds' names are better. Cuckoo—sockeroo. Magpie—that really grabs me. Wish I chewed a piece right now."

"If I had my notebook I'd make you a poem, Crash Adams. I'd dip my finger in blood and . . ."

"If you had your notebook, I'd have my pie. Back at the kayak. Wonder where." I circumnavigated the 'Glades with my eyes, ending up with a tour of our hummock. For the first time I saw a square concrete structure about the size of two outhouses, only not that tall. Right below us, amid felled bushes. Jumbled next to it were piles of palms, cabin timbers, dead animals, and a live one. "Fawn—up against the wall. Nose twitching."

"Where's the mother? I'd speculate she's dead. Drowned."

"Or beaned by a branch."

"Perhaps half-conscious, near here." June freed herself from vines so she could get a better view of our wilderness wasteland.

"Or starved to death. Like me. Like you, if we don't eat. How long's it been?" I felt enormously hungry, surly in my stomach. I glared at the sun. It glared back from directly overhead. Noon. Noon in the eye. We'd eaten when? I tried to recall. Yesterday? Yesterday evening?

June trickled butterflies again. "We shall milk honeysuckle. Sip it."

"All blown away."

Birds thatched June's hair. "We shall gather pond apples right out of the slough."

"Too pulpy for me. Fleshy. I tried one once, over on the Anhinga Trail." Which way, that trail? What direction, civilization? We'd know in minutes as the sun tipped toward afternoon. "Watch the sun, poet. We'll get our bearings."

"I'm hoping to sight the creek where we moored last night. How far did we walk?"

I thought back. I remembered the effort. "We never walked. We pigged it through muck. Maybe a block. Maybe a football field. Who could tell in that cutthroat wind?" My stomach grumbled. I sighed and griped about grub.

June kept right on sweeping her eyes through the eye. Calm, the three. "Say we came a hundred yards to this hummock from Rocky Creek. Or even three hundred. We perhaps could wade over there for supplies."

"Grab cupcakes, your pen and sonnets, the rescue gear, and hustle right here again before Aretha rips our hearts off."

I felt uneasy soon as I said that, for no telling when the hurricane might hound us again. Any second. If we tried for our cupboard we could drown in the high-water sawgrass, be stranded without our tree, our citadel. I leaned my forehead against the silky gumbo limbo. Wind had peeled its papery bark, stripped its leaves, severed many branches, but still it survived. Would we?

I shut my eyes. I got this vision of me and June engulfed by a tidal wave, razed by a tornado. The putrid smell of rotting animals arose from piled bodies. I sniffed death. My vision worsened. Every sort of natural disaster beset the Everglades: hot molten lava mired our feet, siroccos sapped our strength. Forest fires turned us to charcoal, and our bodies fell into earthquake fissures, there wolfed down by wolves, bears, plagues of locusts and fire ants.

And alligators. Alligatored down.

I'd heard a bellow in my trance. I unwedged myself from the tree crotch for an unobstructed view up, down.

"Where?" asked June. She knew the sound.

"I'm hunting. Just a second. Everything's covered with storm droppings."

"Not his tail."

Flamp. Flamp. Flamp. Against our castle. A tail at the moat. "That's a biggie. He can't climb, though, so don't be alarmed."

"I'm not. He's looking elsewhere. Toward the fawn by the cistern."

"You mean that cement outhouse? A cistern? Not like MacMaster's down in the Keys. Theirs is round and much taller."

What else could it be? I wondered. Before Aretha it must have stood beside our smithereened shack, catching water from the roof—a sort of above-the-ground well. Now it stood alone, silvery walls mostly hidden by debris. The fawn cowered in the shade, watching the huge alligator draw within jaw range.

"Crash, we can't let it happen. He'll eat . . ."

"Better a haunch of venison than morsels of Regan and Adams. That fellow'll fill himself on deer and leave us alone in case we fall on him later."

"I won't look." I heard her breathing quicken and felt her touch urge me away from the snap. "Turn away," she commanded.

"June, you're too tender. Don't be a baby." I fixed my eyes on the scene ten feet under us. The alligator swam toward his lunch, reached the debris island, climbed slowly up its frond and plank planks, padded across trash, unclamped his jaws, and—

I turned away. I hid my face on June's shoulder. I wanted to stop my ears but was afraid to let go of the tree. I heard a thrashed tail, a low bleat, June's "Oh no," and a mighty SNAP.

But not an ivory clicksnap. More like metal clanksnapping. Steel teeth gnashing once.

"I can't look," I said to June's collarbone. My sick, rocking stomach warned me away from the meal below. Alligator bellows blistered the silence. "Don't talk with your teeth full, you green monster," I called through a tongueful of jacket, dry nylon now. Huge slapping sounds—tail against water—rocked the hummock.

"He's not eating. He's being eaten," June whispered.

I clenched my eyes tighter. I burrowed my head.

"He's caught in a trap."

I didn't look.

"He's locked in an open-air dungeon. Oh, the poor dragon."

Still, I didn't look. I glanced up at June's eyes. Wide open and pinned to the ground, they sprang tears enough for both of us. Her saltwater splashed my lashes. I flinched and finally peeked down.

Caught in a trap, all right—the alligator, not the deer. A huge set of rusty iron teeth encircled his armored midriff. Whew! How he must hurt! "That's a bear trap, Regan. Could have been set in this hummock. Or swept here by Aretha One."

"We're fortunate not to have stepped into it last night," June answered, crying more.

"Better his hide than ours."

Yet I pitied that great beast. As he bucked and thumped to shuck off iron I felt close to him, a fellowship as our own doom blew nearer—Aretha II. "I'd free that big guy if I knew how," I called over his death rattle. I looked away again. I trailed the fawn in full flight west, toward the afternoon sun.

"I know you would, Crash."

"I'm not strong enough to pry apart those pinchers. If Rollie were here . . ."

"She isn't strong enough either."

"I know." Besides, I thought, she'd be laughing.

"At least the deer escaped," we said in one breath.

We watched him bound through the sawgrass, water at times to his neck. Moments later, a hundred yards west, he disappeared completely. For

seconds. Then, head up, out of—out of Rocky
Creek, he swam. "You're right, June. We aren't far
from Number One. I think I hear your pencil calling. Singing to you from your laundry bag."

"A duet with Rollie's fudge." June began to
ease herself down from her perch. We both did,
tangles for helpers.

I hit the hummock first. "I'll struggle over there,
gather what we . . ."

"I'll come with you."

"No need. Stay and dry."

"Crash, we're in business together, the business
of keeping alive. I'm with you."

"Then follow me into the sun."

I sloshed a path. June waded in my wake for a
while, then came abreast. The water was comfort-
ably warm, the sawgrass not so slashing as before.
In that gold and green afternoon we might as well
have been on a spree. I scooped clear water on
June. She scooped back. I ducked for a sip, spit
past her smile. Her mouthful streamed by mine.
She prodded me with water lilies. I stole them,
strung them on blades of sawgrass, slung this tiara
on June's brown hair. "You can have some fun in
the eye," I said in a mood of third-degree happi-
ness. We romped to our heart's content.

Right up to the ledge where #1 wasn't.

"I had my heart set on getting your notebook
so's you could write us a poem in the tree—right
from storm experience. No more second-hand
stuff."

June looked distressed. Her eyes mourned our

kayak. "Matches gone. I wanted to build a fire on a stump in our hummock, cook you lunch."

"Let's poke among the mangroves here. Maybe Number One's hiding in the roots."

Such clumps to search! Such gobs of sawgrass to mow with our eyes! All the rocks were awash, the creek peppered with spiky palmetto fans, pine bark, wisps of blue vinyl, a paperback swollen to family-Bible size. "Our folboat's been around," I said, hefting *Poets and Poems* when it ran aground on an abandoned anthill. "Here ya go, June, your rescue kit." She squeezed it and looked more.

Until she found her duffle, tied to the seat back that was tied to her life jacket. The whole works all gloppy. She grubbed it up, though, and continued to beat the bulrushes. "Your food," she said, "comes next."

But it didn't. We played water polo with various other crushed objects from our ex-boat, drank wolfishly from Rocky Creek, consulted the sky for a sign of death, turned hinders to the sun, and backtracked. With our tree before us, we hurried now. We moved clownishly, like a pair of drunks or spastics, what with toting that load of soaked books and clawing our feet from the marsh bottom. Plus, the wind began to rise rapidly. The atmosphere turned copper-colored, then darkened. Lightning led us east, the first bolt miles away—over Miami Beach, maybe. The second came closer, louder, lower; the third neared our hummock as we did.

"That tree's no good for shelter," I hollered, fifteen yards from the goal. "Lightning seeks tall . . ."

A fourth bolt sizzled directly ahead. I scrammed down, tasted soil, upped to butt June, who was pointing through the boiling-black sky at a column of fire: our gumbo limbo, a torch now, guiding us to higher ground.

Guiding us to the cistern. The flimsy lid gave with one push, allowing plenty of space for June's slim self to drop in, enough for my wider hips to breach. Standing almost necks deep in rainwater, we reached and eased the cover over us again.

"It's called a water bed," June cried through the almost-human howls of Aretha II. "A vertical one."

"Poet, you've got a knack of making the best of things. Can you write under water, too?"

Our laughter rang around the cistern, merged with the killer storm . . .

JUNE 5th

ALL AFTERNOON

and died.

"So dank here."

Redoubled rain maddened the hummock.

"Never mind. We're safe. Cement won't blow,"
I blustered.

"That remains to be seen."

Ravening wind convulsed the Everglades.

"How much more of this?"

"All afternoon. Like all morning." June's answer
calm.

"Equal sides to the worst part of a hurricane?"

"Most probably."

We stood together under seige.

"Oh, June, can we bear it?"

"We will."

Dots of dim light seeped through the lid.

"Aretha's busting our cover."

"Eventually she'll pull it off."

"I hurt in a coupla new places."

At hand, June's duffle floated on its life jacket.

"Read to me. Pass time."

"I will. I've my extra glasses."

"A story poem. Once-upon-a-timer."

"I prefer lyrics."

"Not metaphors. Not similes. Can't keep them straight."

"Poems need images. For strength. For beauty."

"For exams I write definitions on my palm: 'like,' 'as.' "

"Don't trouble with definitions. Poems are feelings. Feel them."

"Read. I'll feel them."

"I'll write, too, by and by. About us. All this."

June read.

"An awful tempest mashed the air
The clouds were gaunt and few . . ."

"Like up there," I broke in.

"I had been hungry all the years
My noon had come to dine . . ."

"Like me. Like now."

"Safe in their alabaster chambers
Untouched by morning and untouched by noon . . ."

"What's an 'alabaster chamber'?"

"A tomb."

"Like us. Like here."

"My river runs to thee
Blue sea, wilt welcome me . . ."

"Dickinson? All of those?"

"You found me drowning, caught my hair
Alas, you sought to break my nose . . ."

"Sounds like Dickinson but it's Regan this time. Right?"

Then Regan, Regan, Regan with upcraned neck, scribbling on the white cement.

"Write in your own voice. Don't imitate."

"I will."

"You're June, not Emily."

The glare of almost perpetual lightning revealed her words.

"Cistern graffiti."

"Do you like my title: 'Poet to Crash'?"

That the rain tried to erase when our cover twisted up and away.

"Ink would wash off. This pencil sticks."

"I trust it won't lead-poison this drinking water."

"Poetry can't pollute."

Raindrops like shotputs scourged our well. Water deepened.

"Rise is all it does." I began to tread.

"We could use some stilts."

"Take off your belt. I'll buckle ours together."

"Here."

"Now around, under your arms."

"You won't have to hold my mouse hair this time."

"It's thick. Foxhair . . ."

Which the vast churning wind circle tried to root out.

"Are there leeches in my scalp?"

"No, June, only Aretha Two. Bloodsucking wind's ganging up on us."

I fixed her head firmly in the crook of my elbow.

"We've other company, Crash."

"Who? Where?" I treaded for us both.

"Snake on the ledge—above."

Fright tried to tighten my skin. But couldn't anymore.

"A shortie. It would take more than that . . ."

"And slender. But 'summer's treason,' remember?"

Gooseflesh tried to pop through mosquito bites. But didn't again.

"Hues like a rainbow."

"Colorfuller than those last killers."

"Rings of red, yellow . . ."

The cistern held back my fear.

"A deadly coral snake, Rollie's cobra." I stayed steady.

"Black, pinkish yellow."

"He wouldn't dive in here? He'd drown?"

"We'll rise to him with the water level."

Rain washed "I don't care" from my mouth, then slackened.

"My legs are spent. Been treading for hours."

"I'll take over," June said. "I promise."

"No, I'll hoist us out of here. Wind's down."

"Wind's died."

JUNE 5th to 6th

EVENING, MORNING,
NOON AND NIGHT

My snakebite hadn't even hurt. I didn't feel a fang strike. I felt a chew from tiny teeth, almost a gum munch. I didn't cry out. Instead I said, "June, he got me," very quiet, and kept on pulling against the ledge, drawing myself from the water. Then I helped June up. For so long we'd been close to drowning in that cistern, both too exhausted to pedal, thrash, tread longer. In a reflex I reached for the ledge and—nip, nosh from that little guy.

"Where? Let me look?"

"Right trigger finger. He just sort of wiggled quick, sidled up to my paw, and pinpricked me. I saw what happened better than I felt it. He had such funny eyes—almost touching."

I put my hand, shrivelly from hours in water, into June's two shriveled ones. She turned it over and over in the waning light. She bent close to the finger. "I find no punctures. Are you sure?"

"Of course I'm sure. I watched that black bullet snout do its thing." I grabbed my hand, held it up to the clouds, and searched. "Right on the tip. There."

"Oh, my poor Crash, you're right." She took my hand again, thrust it in the waist-deep water of our hummock. "First I'd better wash off any poison left on the skin before it flows into these little holes. No sense in letting you become worse. Does it tingle? Feel sore?"

"No more than a bee sting. Almost not at all right now. Maybe some harmless snake resembles the coral?"

June took off her glasses.

"Or maybe I'm immune to venom."

June broke one lens against the cistern, carefully catching the glass chips.

"No pain of any sort. What are you up to?"

"Cut and suck. Standard snakebite procedure."

With that she raked a sliver twice across both punctures, making bloody X's. She squeezed these cuts hard until the water frothered pink around us. "Now it hurts, all right," I yelped.

"I feel it with you, Crash. But without antivenin our best hope is to keep as much poison as possible from the bloodstream." She began sucking my fingertip. Deep dimples appeared on her cheeks from strain. "Your blood's so warm . . . salty . . . tastes like carrots. Or maybe wild tamarind." She spit toward the cistern.

"People die from bites. I've read in the papers. Kids and things."

"You're not 'people.' You're Crash Adams. Strong, brave."

"I'm about sick of being brave."

"You won't die. I won't let you. Wash again."

I dipped my entire arm back in Aretha's handiwork—water as far as twilight sight. With rain stopped, wind only occasional zephyrs, the Everglades lay purple, warm, tranquil, unpeopled—a liquid Eden. Rescuers should be out in force soon, beating the mangroves for two lost Nature, Inc., girls. "June, we should run up a flag on our burned shell of a tree. Your sweater, my shirt, something pale will do. Rangers'll spot it in the morning." She turned her pockets inside out until she came across her handkerchief. "Too tattered and small," I said.

"Not for a tourniquet. Give me back your hand."

"Oh, come off it, June. I keep telling you I'm okay. I'm climbing that tree with my jacket, tying . . ."

"I'm tying on your tourniquet. I mean business. Then you're helping me cover this cistern again so I can make you a bed on top—a real one, this time."

"You're bossier than Rollie."

"Now I have to be with you. Hold still."

I complained and complained as she applied her silly hankie in a Nurse Jane Fuzzywuzzy tourniquet, and I grumbled even more about stacking pieces of our shack across the open cistern. "We should be in our tree, hailing rangers."

"Perhaps one of the symptoms of coral snake bite is crankiness," she answered. "Lie down. Gently, gentle with yourself."

"You're nutty."

"Crash, listen. This bite could be like eating

green apples or too many cherries. You feel fine for several hours after gorging yourself. Then all at once—"

"Gut-wrenching pain. Okay, I'm prone and waiting."

June emptied her laundry bag next to me, stuck a bloated dictionary under my feet, the life preserver under my head, and for a long time waded around the hummock collecting leaves, grass, fronds for a browse bed. She called to me from time to time. I watched, then I didn't. I couldn't. My eyelids began to droop, and when I attempted to kick the book away I felt weak and out of breath.

"Crash, please keep your feet elevated. It's a way to combat shock." June hovered over me, stuffing her duffle with the wet collection. "Browse mattress. Lift yourself."

I wasn't able to. My mind told my back to inch up but it stayed put. Yet I couldn't seem to care. I felt no anxiety about being helpless. Instead I felt sort of happy. Giddy. I tittered like an imbecile and said, "You   lift   me   for   a change."

Remarkably, she did. A leg, an arm, a back at a time. "You're dead weight, Crasher. What's the matter?" She pushed and tugged, nestling my body in the browse-bed.

"I . . . I . . ." I giggled like old Janet.

"From a crosspatch to a laughing girl in half an hour. What an extremist you are." She sat next to me, released the tourniquet, soaked blood in a mauve rag torn from her blouse, and asked, "Shall

I read to you again? Out of one eye through my one lens left? We've less than an hour of light."

My drooping eyes must have said "Yes," for June unstuck pages of a volume and reeled off poem after poem. About nature. About olden times. About feelings. About love. She skipped the death ones. I could hear all right. I could see darkness closing down on us. I felt mosquitoes clinging to my cheeks and smelled—miraculously—bananas somewhere near. Nothing wrong with my senses. But along about the millionth poem I could feel a weight pressing on my chest, like maybe a great yacht had cruised up and parked on me. I labored for air.

June swished away mosquitoes and laid a cool hand on my forehead. "We need light—a fire. So I can tend you."

"So   mosquitoes   will   bug   off." Words came hard to me for the first time in my life. I heard June splashing water, then noticed her fingers kneading my face, neck, forearms, my legs through tears in cloth.

"Mud. Thick. Keeps insect stingers from penetrating your skin. Rollie's solution, remember? Crash, stay awake!"

"I   am.   I   am."

"Please don't lose the trick of it. Hang tough."

"The   fires.   Put   out   the   fires."

"Fires? Crash are you burning up? Should I sprinkle water on you? How's this? Nod, please nod. Are you awake? Crash, please stay awake. If you can . . . if you don't go into shock . . . if you can survive the night we're bound to be rescued.

You'll get antivenin. Oh Crash, stay alive. Let me
hold your eyes open so you'll see Venus all silvery
white—our evening star. Look, it blossoms from
the clouds. Watch. Don't shut your gaze down.
Don't go into eclipse with Venus rising. The stars
will console you. We've no moon at all yet, no
moonflowers after wild days. But our wild nights
are over. Tomorrow / given life / we'll wear sun /
eat stems and petals / tap roots for . . ."

"Uncle."

"Poet,   you   made   morning   happen."
"I'll organize some breakfast."
"My   stomach.   Nausea."
"You've nothing to throw up. No meals yester-
day. I'll fetch pond apples. 'Starve a fever, feed a
snakebite,' I always say."

I breathed the best I could, considering the bat-
tleship docked on my rib cage. While I heaved for
air I listened to June probe the sunny Everglades.
She returned with a cargo of wild bananas, peeled
me one, and held it to my mouth.

"The trees knew that hurricane. They've thrown
fruit in every nook of this hummock. Here. Bite,
bananamouth."

I tried to lift my head. No up. I tried to lift an
arm. No hope. I tried to swallow the small lump
June placed between my lips. "C   a   n   '   t."

"Don't just teethe on it, Crash. Down it."

My tongue stumbled on the fruit. My striving
throat locked. I trembled, then shook as if caught
by a twister. Aretha III? Involuntarily I rolled from

side to side on my pallet. June came beside me, held me down with frightening strength. I tumbled to her. "Y   o   u . . ."

"Convulsions. They go along with poisonings. Once I saw a mouse shake himself to death after eating poisoned bait. You must stop. Tell your muscles to stay still. Tell them. Tell them! Mind over body. I'll help. My mind, too."

Right away she pressed me to the planks until, seizure over, I lay in a haze of suffering. Shooting pains around the bite made my eyes brim. Abdominal cramps forced tears sideways through my lids. Cells athirst for air, I wept for the first time in . . .

Noon again now. Our sixth noon. The sun watched me dying with my dumb wet eyes open. Water seemed stretched forever around me. I heard June's voice from a distance: "Tinder. Kindling." A plane, invisible, motored overhead. A vulture, visible, perched heavily on the blackened gumbo limbo. I smelled smoke. June, again at hand, answered my eyes. "Fire, with this mirror in the change purse Mom gave me Monday. I hadn't even looked in it to comb my hair. Sun looked, though, and started our brush bonfire. On piled stumps. Marsh-grass tinder. I blew it like Aretha. Bark kindling. That search-plane pilot will see us now." She held the mirror to my mouth, knelt close, and examined it for moist breath. "Crash, breathe. It's do or die now."

By turns playful, solemn, shouting poems,

hushed, affectionate, bullying, June tried to nudge me to life. I felt her stout-hearted effort but my lassitude worsened. I gave up, gave out of breath. The mirror remained unclouded.

Then her hands stretched to my chest plate and she was pressing, pressing, pressing my heart. She applied the heel of one hand to the heel of the other, massaging in a steady rhythm. She used her body weight, bore down, eased up, bore down, eased up, rested, put her ear to my heart and listened, checked the mirror, bore down, eased up. "Come back, Crash. From wherever you are." Bore down. "Back." Eased up. "Back." Bore down. "Come back." Eased up. "Back to me."

Until my heart banged blood. Until, spontaneously, I gasped, coughed, inhaled, gulped the poet's "Back / Brush death / Bite life / Blink time . . ."

Under another Venus, our fire roared in the dark. June fed it branches, me small nips of fruit —tokens of Aretha. I knew peace. "We've never been lost all along," I said finally over the distant clip of an airboat.

"Here I am," shouted June above the boat's approaching sawmill noise.

"Here we are," I whispered.

Its search lights roved our watery garden.

"They've sighted us, Crash."

"I   see   them."

"There's Rollie pointing from the deck. She's found us."

"We've   found   us," I whispered again.
Aloud I said, "She doesn't seem as tall."

"Here we are!"

"We're out of it."

Oh, the joy.

JUNE 7th

From the jaw of the Lostmans you pulled me,
And you bit me.
When, by teeth of the innocent wilderness,
Bitten you lay,
I sucked your death away.
Great Nature's necessitous anger!
On all the beasts and us she howled and rained.
We took turns in courage
And our rescue gained.
Oh, the dear air
Of the after-storm, and our care
In the circle of our friends,
As we lie lax-limbed and tell
Our perilous, our sinuous adventure,
But not how it ends—
No, not how it ends.

"At last George Plimpton has been out Plimptoned.
Gloria Steinem has met her match.
Joe Namath can retire and rest his sore knees."

HAL HIGDON

Zanballer

R. R. KNUDSON

Suzanne Hagen wanted nothing to do with cheer-leading, baton twirling or folkdancing. She wanted to play ball; and if boys could play football, why not girls? Zan's remarkable gridiron career began when her principal closed down the gym for repairs and forced the girls to participate in such unsporting activities as folk dancing. In revolt, Zan led them out of dance class and onto the football field, where they formed a team called Catch-11 and began their uphill run to football glory.

A LAUREL-LEAF LIBRARY BOOK $1.25

8819-04

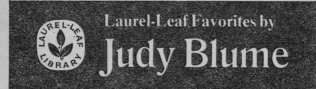

Laurel-Leaf Favorites by
Judy Blume

☐ **ARE YOU THERE GOD? IT'S ME, MARGARET**
After moving from the city to a new home in the suburbs, 11-year-old Margaret faces the challenges of making new friends, getting along with boys, growing up physically—and choosing a religion. $1.25 (90419-6)

☐ **BLUBBER**
Fifth-grader Jill Brenner tells how the kids in her class abuse another classmate, Linda Fischer. $1.25 (90707-1)

☐ **DEENIE**
Deenie liked to feel pretty and resented any nagging about her poor posture. Then she learned that she had adolescent idiopathic scoliosis—and that she would have to wear a back and hip brace for at least four years. $1.25 (93259-9)

☐ **STARRING SALLY J. FREEDMAN AS HERSELF**
Set in Miami Beach, in 1947, this story depicts the adventures of Sally J. Freedman's close and loving Jewish family as they adjust to their first winter in Florida. $1.50 (98239-1)

☐ **THEN AGAIN, MAYBE I WON'T**
His father's sudden wealth creates problems for 13-year-old Tony Miglione, involving his family, his new community, and growing up. $1.25 (98659-1)

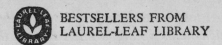

BESTSELLERS FROM LAUREL-LEAF LIBRARY

☐ **ARE YOU THERE, GOD? IT'S ME, MARGARET**
by Judy Blume $1.25 0419-39

☐ **THE BOY WHO COULD MAKE HIMSELF
DISAPPEAR** by Kin Platt $1.25 0837-25

☐ **THE CHOCOLATE WAR**
by Robert Cormier $1.25 4459-08

☐ **DEENIE** by Judy Blume $1.25 3259-02

☐ **DURANGO STREET**
by Frank Bonham $1.25 2183-13

☐ **FAIR DAY, AND ANOTHER STEP BEGUN**
by Katie Letcher Lyle $1.25 5968-09

☐ **IF I LOVE YOU, AM I TRAPPED FOREVER?**
by M. E. Kerr $1.25 4320-05

☐ **I'LL GET THERE, IT BETTER BE
WORTH THE TRIP** by John Donovan ... $1.25 3980-08

☐ **I'M REALLY DRAGGED BUT NOTHING
GETS ME DOWN** by Nat Hentoff .... 95¢ 3988-26

☐ **I WILL GO BAREFOOT ALL SUMMER FOR YOU**
by Katie Letcher Lyle $1.25 4327-08

☐ **JANE EMILY** by Patricia Clapp .... 75¢ 4185-09

☐ **THE OUTSIDERS** by S. E. Hinton $1.25 6769-40

☐ **THE PIGMAN** by Paul Zindel $1.25 6970-11

☐ **THAT WAS THEN, THIS IS NOW**
by S. E. Hinton $1.25 8652-12

At your local bookstore or use this handy coupon for ordering: